CLOWN BOY

By Andy Nibley

Jules,
Really value your
friendship & wisdom.
Let me know
what you think.

Andy

This book is dedicated to Gower Nibley.

I owe a debt of gratitude to Kelly Colbert, Bob Crooke, Janie Gabbett and Frank Gilbert for all their support and encouragement as I wrote this book over the years.

Chapter One

Dylan didn't cry when she died.

He didn't actually cry until they sang *Amazing Grace*, and even then, he didn't cry for her. He cried because all the voices were too loud, too discordant, too much for his muddled little mind to make sense of.

His mother had been dead for days, yet he had not once shown even the slightest sign that he was moved by her passing, at least, not in a way that any normal human being could comprehend.

No, he didn't seem to really understand or really care about what was going on around him; he didn't seem to care, that is, until the people who had come to honor his mother, the people who filled up the massive stone cathedral that soared above his head, began to sing in her memory. Then he broke down, really broke down, reduced to a sea of tears, tears of fear, tears of real pain.

"Stop it! Stop it!" he screamed at the top of his lungs, interrupting the memorial service, causing scores of heads to whip around to see what was going on, craning to find out what new tragedy had befallen the Bonner clan.

"You stop it," I whispered loudly to Dylan, grabbing my son sternly by the arm. "You stop it now!"

But my boy was unraveling too fast, coming apart at the seams, melting down in a hurry. "Make them stop, Daddy!" he wailed. "Make them stop singing. Make them stop NOW!"

The singing ceased. There was total silence save the echo of the air vents blowing through the hallowed halls of the gargantuan granite church. I looked into Dylan's porcelain blue eyes, straining to see what my child was feeling, straining to see what was going on inside that gorgeous tow-head of his.

"Make them stop, Daddy," a quivering Dylan repeated softly, unaware the singing had already stopped, tears welling up in his eyes, eyes that were just like hers, eyes that were begging "make it all go away."

"They have stopped, Dylan," I said gently, bending down to hug him. "They have stopped, son. They've stopped singing."

Ignoring, as best I could, my suffocating, chest-crushing sorrow, I turned to the assembled crowd of friends and associates, people whom my wife, Letitia and I had known, for years. The silence was deafening.

"Perhaps we could skip that song," I said. "Maybe we could just skip singing altogether."

I could see all of them, but especially the women, my mother,

her mother, all of them looking at me, with tears of their own, great, giant tears of their own. And I knew what they were thinking. They were thinking: how the hell is this guy ever going to be able to take care of that kid? How is that "I never want to grow up" comedian, that professional clown boy, going to be able to take care of a kid like that, a confused, mixed up, eight-year-old kid like that? Lettie did everything for those two. And now she's gone. What will become of them, what will happen to them? It's so sad, they were all thinking, it's just so sad.

Well, fuck them, I thought to myself. Fuck them, but good. It's sad alright, sad on a scale that I couldn't have imagined humanly possible only a few days ago. But somehow, I had clawed my way through the pain and the heart-break, minute by minute, hour by hour, day by day, hung in there until the funeral, hung in there until she could be laid to rest.

With all the firmness at my command, I took hold of Dylan's hand. Don't worry, son. We'll figure it out. Somehow, we'll figure it out.

But Dylan was already drifting away. Something spectacular, something intriguing, had lit up his still developing brain, dimmed his eyes to the outside world, taken him away from this terrible place, this terrible funeral, this terrible world, taken him to wherever it was that he went all the time, that place where he lived great chunks of his life, that place where I could never go.

"How many of you out there tonight are women?"

It was the way I started all my shows, all of my gigs. It was a trick of my own device, a trick that let me know what kind of audience was out there, beyond the blinding bright lights, beyond the first row, out there in the dark shadows, out there where my eyes could not penetrate.

I knew that if there were a lot of high pitched "woo-hoo's" after my opening gambit, then the audience was predominantly young and female. If there were a few, more measured shouts of encouragement, I knew the crowd was older, but still primarily female.

If there were no hoots or hollers, I knew the folks out there were probably men and men are the worst audiences, by far. All they ever want to hear are jokes about dicks and pussy. The younger men are particularly tough. They are usually out on cheap dates. Pay the $15 cover. Get the girl drunk. Take her home.

I always pray for a female audience. I can generally do my more sophisticated stuff with women, my more thoughtful material, political humor, current events jokes, stuff like that.

With a room full of men, I usually just write off the whole evening from the start, pack it in, tell a few dirty jokes, not dirty dirty jokes, but a little bit more salacious jokes than usual, and then work on my timing and delivery, and hope that my 10 minutes on stage will go by as quickly as possible.

Tonight was going to be one of those nights, one of those dreadful nights, a men's night. The joint was full of them, mostly "bridge and tunnel" guys, in their 20s mostly, from Jersey and Long Island.

"I don't want to say I'm the product of a broken home, but my father has been married and divorced so many times, that when he goes down to the Manhattan court house, he doesn't have to wait in line to get through security like the rest of us..." I paused for effect, setting up the punch line. *"Naw, he goes down there so much, the judges all chipped in and got him an E-Z Pass."*

A handful of guffaws, only a couple of serious laughs, but none of them from the belly. They were waiting for the pussy jokes.

I hate kowtowing to audiences. I can do jokes about the difference between men and women, the never-ending battle of the sexes, sure. And I am not above throwing in a few cuss words here and there. But even during my most trying nights, I steadfastly refuse to go all the way down into the gutter, become a pure smut machine, just to get a few cheap laughs.

That's probably why I'll never make it big. That's probably why I'll be playing these seedy dives until the day I die.

But it was too late to change my routine now, even if I wanted to. The comedy roller coaster had left the platform. Once a routine is chosen – and I always have three to choose from depending on which of the three demographics I identify with my opening line -- there is no turning back. Once a particular path is chosen, once I have committed to it, I can't shut it down.

Just because I was in a surly mood, I picked the routine for older women even though the crowd reeked of millennial maleness.

"My pop's shrink said to him just this week... Mr. Bonner have you learned anything... anything at all... from being married to all those women?"

I paused again, setting up another punch line. Timing is everything in comedy.

"Yeah, doc, Dad said... I've learned it's not a real good idea to refer to your current wife... as... your current *wife."*

Nervous laughter. Some coughs. One long, knowing chuckle from a divorced woman, somewhere in the dark, somewhere out there in the back, left-hand corner of the room. Thank God for her.

Comedy makes no sense. Some nights they pee in their pants, fall out of their chairs. The next night, same routine, same club, same jokes, same timing. Nothing. You can hear a pin drop. The longest 10 minutes of your life.

Why do I do this? Why do I subject myself to this torture, this indignation? Night after night. I don't really have a choice. It's what I do. It's who I am.

"A lot of people called my father the town drunk, and I won't deny he had his drinking problems," I barged ahead. *"But I'll tell you this, he was a family man, a real family man. Every Sunday morning, he would gather the family together in the living room and then we would go out and look for the car... together... as a family."*

And so it went, another night in the trenches, another night of wondering whether I was the biggest loser to ever hit this planet, or if I was so pathetic I couldn't even claim that title.

Another night of comedy.

Chapter Two

I remember when Lettie first came home and told me that she thought something was wrong with Dylan, that she thought there was something seriously amiss with our son. The boy was four at the time.

“Lance,” she said to me in the way she did when she wanted me to pay attention, close attention, and not clown around. “Dylan is different from the other kids he plays with. I think we may need to get him some help.”

"That's the problem with you people," I snapped at her, as if she were the enemy. "Everybody in this world is terrified of anyone who is unique, anyone who does not conform to their standards, anyone who is not just like them."

Lettie knew what was coming. She had seen the movie many, many times before. She knew what was in store even before she walked in the door. Even so, she waited patiently, waited patiently while I got my rant on, and out.

"Do you know that Van Gogh only sold one painting in his whole life? One stinking painting. The greatest artist of all time sold one painting," I burnt with rage, my voice getting louder and louder. "His brother bought it for eight bucks, eight bucks, out of pity. He felt sorry for him."

I was out of control, ripped, scorching with unbridled indignation.

"That's how much humanity knows about creativity, about genius, about anyone who is different. Fuck everybody and fuck what they think of our son. We don't need their pity. We don't need them to feel sorry for him. We don't need their eight bucks."

Tears welled up in Lettie's eyes, her sweet, sensitive aqua blue eyes, eyes just like Dylan's.

"You know that they tried to flunk Einstein out of high school, don't you?" I was not going to cave in now, not going to let her tears get to me. "That's how much people know about genius. The smartest man who ever lived and they wanted to kick him out of school. Stupid bastards, stupid, self-absorbed, full of shit bastards..."

But I was running out of steam. I knew that she had heard this rant, this foaming at the mouth before, so many times before. I knew that she knew the routine, backwards and forward, every word of it. Why was I doing this to her again?

I finally stopped and took my tiny, visibly shaken, beloved wife into my arms. "Sorry," I whispered. I could smell the essence of her, the love, the kindness. "I'm really sorry."

Lettie collapsed into a heap of uncontrollable sobs. I could feel the softness of her back through her cotton print dress. She was trembling, frightened and inconsolable.

There was nothing I could do, at this point, nothing I could do except hold onto my wife for dear life, and try to keep from opening my dumb-ass trap again.

It was the unfairness of it, the randomness of it that made Lettie's death so hard to take. There was no reason for her to die. She hadn't done anything wrong. She never did anything wrong.

She was just minding her own business, walking down Second Avenue in the Lower East Village, taking a stroll on a perfect autumn day. That's when the cab jumped a curb to avoid a head-on with a drunk driver who had illegally turned right into oncoming, one-way traffic.

There was no time for Lettie to think, to move, to do anything. They say she died almost instantly, pinned up against the brick wall of an Ethiopian restaurant that no one ever went to.

Smashed to bits, a grotesque collage of crushed bone, torn tissue and flesh, and buckets of splattered blood, heaved up against the wall of that customer-less joint, that fucking worthless joint, on an idyllic Monday afternoon in New York City. So senseless, so meaningless, so incredibly unfair.

The two vehicles were totaled, but the cab driver and the drunk driver weren't hurt too badly. They were both carted off to the hospital for observation and released a couple of hours later on their own recognizance.

Lettie was not released from the hospital a few hours later. She was not released on her own recognizance.

She had been taken from me without fair restitution, because there is no such thing as fair restitution when the woman you love, the only woman who ever meant anything at all to you, has been taken away, taken away for good.

The first time I met Letitia, I was mopping up near the spinach stand in the vegetable section at *Trader Joe's*, the one down on 14th Street, around the corner from Union Square. I was the day manager there, making more than the minimum wage, but only enough to live in a tiny Flatbush apartment, barely able to support myself, much less anyone else.

She was dressed smartly, in a black, neatly tailored outfit, with a necklace of white pearls lovingly strung around her pale neck, looking for all the world like one of those with-it girls who used to be on *Sex and The City*.

Somebody had knocked over a whole pile of organic spinach and a whole carton of balsamic vinegar dressing as well. A bunch of bottles had been broken in the process. It was a mess. Spinach and slimy oil everywhere. I was cleaning it up when I looked up from my crouching position and noticed Lettie trying to get around me. Actually, the first thing I noticed were those incredible legs of hers, legs sheathed in a sexy pair of black nylon stockings. As my pal Donnelly would say, what a set of wheels!

"It's good for the eyes," she said. "At least that's what they say."

What? Had she noticed me staring at her gorgeous gams?

"Eating the spinach," she smiled, fully aware of what I had been looking at. "It's good for the eyes. It prevents macular degeneration, or at least, retards it."

She was a minx, all slender and willowy, perfectly proportioned, with flawless posture, pale skin, jet black hair, and blue eyes that lit up the room. Whoa, baby!

It suddenly occurred to me that I, in stark contrast, was wearing a greasy, grime-stained apron, a torn T-shirt, soiled blue jeans, and a *Trader Joe's* baseball cap. Can you spell L-O-S-E-R?

"Well, I guess, the eyes have it," I said clumsily, immediately wishing I had said something a little cleverer.

She gave me a sideways look, a perplexed, but confident glance.

"Yeah, actually, I do," I blurted out, reading her thoughts. "I actually do think I'm a comedian."

She just stared at me, trying to figure out what my game was. So I just kept on going, praying I wasn't making a complete ass out of myself.

"To the untrained, naked eye, it looks like I'm just another produce guy at your local grocery store. But I'm actually here practicing my stand-up comedy routine, underground, undercover, trying to suss out incredibly attractive women and get them to overlook my obvious flaws and fall in love with my sense of humor."

I popped my patented Jack O' Lantern grin, and asked her, pleadingly: "Is it working?"

While I was waiting for her to respond, it occurred to me that I was trying to pick someone up who was out of my league, someone who was absolutely gorgeous. I was making a total fool of myself.

But all of a sudden, she smiled, didn't laugh, just smiled. And there was just a trace of a smirk, a cute little smirk, the kind that girls do that drives guys crazy.

"Really?" she said, mockingly suspicious. "A comedian?"

"Yeah," I smiled back. "Really."

Actually, it was only a little bit of a lie.

The preceding week, I had done my first open mike performance at a dive bar in midtown. No need to tell her how that went. No need to tell her that there was a reason why I was still leaning on a mop in a grocery store.

Chapter Three

One day, when he was a little boy, when we were sitting in the living room, staring at the television set, Dylan blurted out, "Daddy, does furniture think?"

I was caught off guard, but ecstatic, over the moon. What a great fucking question!

I could see out of the corner of my eyes, that Lettie's eyes were pleading with me. "Just tell him 'no.' Just tell him 'furniture doesn't think.'"

But I couldn't. I just couldn't do it. In fact, I refused to do it.

"Son, the Greeks thought that everything had soul, everything possessed a kind of native intelligence, rocks, trees, dirt, everything. And who knows, maybe they were right," I told Dylan, trying unsuccessfully to engage my son in eye-to-eye contact.

“When you cut open the human body, can you find a thought, or an emotion? No. But is there anything in the world more powerful than a thought, more real than an emotion? Of course not. It doesn’t matter if you can’t see them or touch them; they are the most real, most essential things we have in life. In many ways, they are the only things we have in life. So if you are asking me if furniture can think, if furniture can feel, how the hell do I know? How the hell does anybody know?" I was finished, thoroughly satisfied with the lesson I had just offered my offspring.

But Dylan did not react, did not smile, did not feel compelled to supplement my diatribe with any comment. Instead, he turned his small frame around, and without changing expression, headed for his bedroom, the place where he liked to spend most of his time, a place where he could pace back and forth on the thin squares of the do-it-yourself, store-bought carpet, humming and jabbering away to himself, a place where he could be completely alone, lost in his own special world.

When Dylan disappeared, Lettie looked at me and shook her head. “Why do you do that?” she asked. “Why do you confuse him? Why can’t you just be like a normal dad?”

She had a point. And I had no answer.

I loved that Dylan would sit on my lap a few hours before I went to work every day, and we would watch *Snow White and the Seven Dwarfs* for the 43rd time.

Dylan adored the flick and was absolutely obsessed with Dopey. I tried one time to point out to him that there were six other dwarfs to choose from, but Dylan would have none of it. Dopey was his man, all the way.

That year, for Halloween, Lettie made Dylan a Dopey costume, with the purple cap, the green robe, the brown leather belt, the shoes with the curled up toes. Dylan was enchanted. He didn't get out of that outfit for a year. He wore it everywhere, to school, around the house, to the park, to bed, everywhere.

And on those rare occasions when Lettie and I could finally manage to peel the costume off our son's body, when we just couldn't take its ratty-ness another second, we would stuff it into the washer and dryer, and watch as Dylan stood patiently beside the two vibrating machines, dressed only in his tiny BVDs, waiting until his uniform was ready to come out again.

It always takes me a while to get my bearings in the morning and I can remember one particular morning when I woke up, not quite sure where I was.

I opened my eyes to find Dopey, in all his splendor and glory, a few inches from my face. I didn't know how long my costumed son had been standing there, waiting for me to wake up, two minutes, two hours, two days, who knew?

"Hey, Dopey," I finally grunted, clearing my throat of nightly drool and phlegm. "How's it going?"

Dylan looked at me with total sincerity, staring right into my eyes, and said in his patented monotone: "For the first time in my life, things are finally going my way."

I was flabbergasted. I had no comeback. But it didn't matter. Before I could answer him, Dylan turned on heel, green coat, purple hat, curled up toes and all. He was gone. I didn't know if I should go after him and try to ferret out what my son had meant. What kind of problems could Dylan possibly be having at age five?

Or maybe, I should have just congratulated him, let him know that things were pretty much downhill from here on out. You nail potty-training, son. Then you make it through finger-painting. The rest is pretty simple, just finish school, get a job, meet a girl, tie the knot, have some kids, retire, die, easy stuff really.

I loved these Dylan moments. Nonsensical as they might appear to other people, they were magical to me. Dylan's uniqueness, his blinding honesty, his total lack of materialism or competitiveness gave me such enormous joy.

Now that Lettie is gone, I often think that if I was suddenly condemned for some reason to spend the rest of my life with only one person that I would have to choose Dylan. My son always finds a way to make my life interesting, unique, something special.

Dylan wrote his first two songs, two of only three songs he would ever write, when he was five. Lettie and I gave him a wooden guitar, a little play toy guitar, for Christmas that year, and he used to take it everywhere he went, upstairs, into the bathroom, everywhere.

The first tune came out of the blue, one day in the dead of winter. The weather had been dreary and frigid for days. The planet, at least the part where we lived, was coated in crackly snow and ice, barren and forbidding.

Right after breakfast, without warning, Dylan suddenly started strumming and singing at the top of his lungs: *"Radiator, Radiator, Come on!"* That was the name of the song, and pretty much all of the lyrics that went with it.

That spring, Dylan produced his second effort, a ditty entitled *"Put It On The Couch, Do It!"* The melody was as rough and as raunchy as the title. And once again, those were all the lyrics, although he did insert a strange grunting noise between verses that sounded a lot like two people getting it on. Lettie took this to be a sign that the babysitter was letting Dylan watch a little too much MTV, so she got rid of her, and told the next one that there would be no more television watching during the day.

Dylan didn't pen his next song until many years later.

I heard it for the first time while Dylan was singing to himself in the shower. I had inadvertently stumbled into the bathroom while my pre-pubescent son was getting himself cleaned up before bed.

"A Great Big Party for My Penis!" Dylan belted out behind the plastic shower curtain. The joy and generosity of his voice was infectious and made it impossible for me to do anything but burst out laughing.

Yes, I thought, it is a pretty damn amazing piece of equipment, isn't it, son? One of God's greatest, and funniest, gifts.

Enjoy.

I wasn't sure when Dylan developed his sense of humor, but he definitely had one, even in those early years. The kid rarely smiled, exhibited any emotion at all. The only exception was when he would tell his jokes, his nonsensical and frequently macabre jokes.

Every night, when I would put him to bed, we would go over his day.

"What did you do today?" I would ask in that sing-song voice that all parents use when talking to animals and small children.

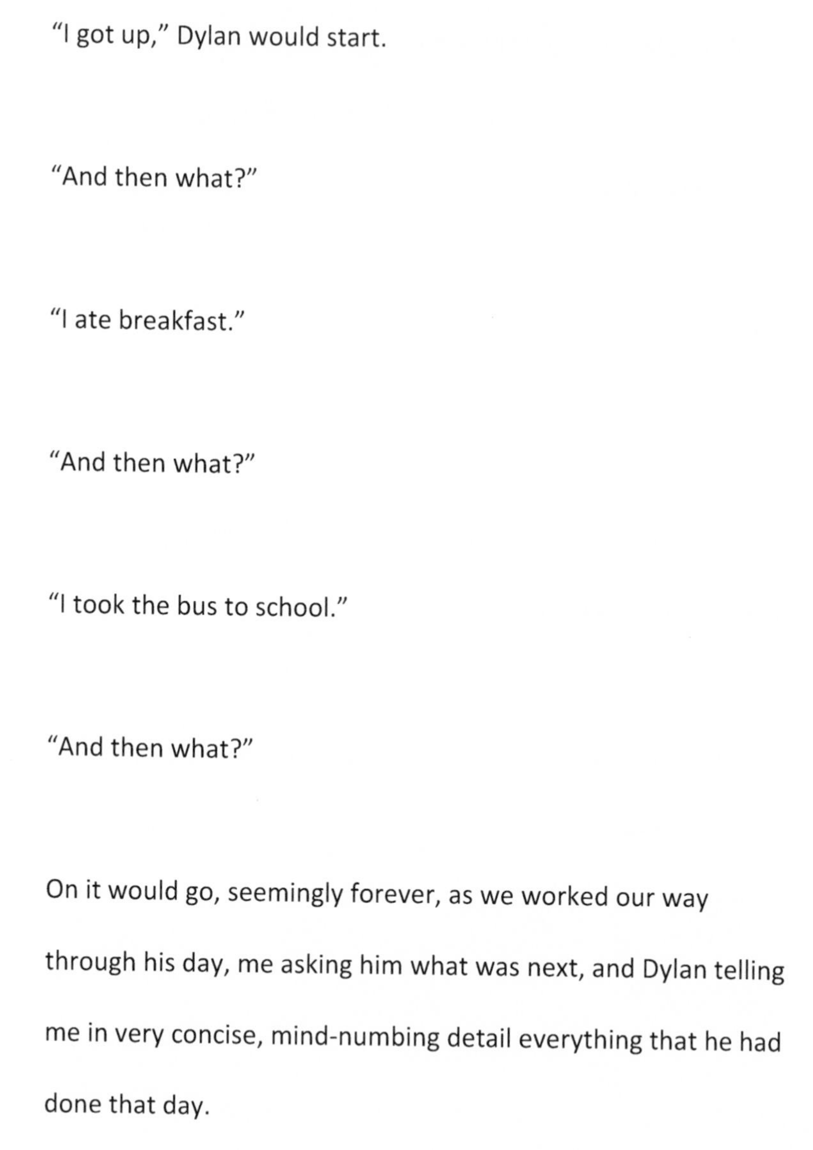

"I got up," Dylan would start.

"And then what?"

"I ate breakfast."

"And then what?"

"I took the bus to school."

"And then what?"

On it would go, seemingly forever, as we worked our way through his day, me asking him what was next, and Dylan telling me in very concise, mind-numbing detail everything that he had done that day.

And when we would finally get to end of his day, after Dylan had told me all about his shower, about brushing his teeth, about the story his teacher had read in school, about the song that Lettie had sung to him before he crawled into bed, after all of that, I would ask him one last time: "And then what?"

Without missing a beat, and with a massive smile on his face, Dylan would shout:

"Then I went swimming in a pool of fire on the roof and did some mushroom lawning!"

At which point, he would dissolve into laughter, uncontrollable, idiotic laughter. And then, so would I. We would fall about, holding our sides, crying till it hurt, father and son in stitches, laughing aloud like a bunch of deranged hyenas.

Sometimes we laughed so long and so hard, Lettie would come in and tell us to shut up, that it was time to go to bed. And then, she would give me that look, that "you're supposed to be the adult here, not another kid encouraging him" look.

And the weird thing was I wasn't even sure what we were laughing about. I just knew that Dylan thought that what he had just said was the funniest thing that he had ever uttered, even if it was the same thing that he said at bedtime every night for months.

At work, I always found something wonderful and delightful and awe-inspiring about any comic who enjoyed his own material no matter how many times he had performed it, a comic who could deliver it night after night, and still get a huge kick out of it. Dylan and his jokes fell comfortably into that category.

Dylan never tired of saying "mushroom lawning," never tired of setting his little joke up, never tired of spitting out the punch line. His timing was always flawless. His delivery was always like he was saying it for the very first time, as if it was as new a joke to him as it was to his listener.

Aside from “mushroom lawning,” Dylan had two other favorites jokes he told.

“Daddy’s car is blue,” he would say with a straight face, quickly adding. “NOT!”

It was a take-off on the old *Saturday Night Live* routine. My car, when I used to have one, was actually red. It wasn’t clear if Dylan actually understood what was funny, or not funny, with the joke, but he was impressed with himself when he saw Lettie and me and anyone else in the room break into smiles whenever he would tell it. That part he definitely got.

“Who’s that walking down the street?” he would ask innocently, cranking up another one of his favorite jokes. And then, smiling like the Cheshire Cat, he would answer: “Abraham Lincoln.” He thought this was hilarious, a real knee-slapper. Because Dylan exhibited happiness and joy so infrequently, Lettie and I were always delighted when he found something to laugh about.

Another thing that really amuses Dylan is when he makes a mistake, any kind of a mistake, but particularly if he misspells or mispronounces something. Add to this his very morbid fascination, humor-wise, with death and destruction, and you have a winning formula.

So possibly, the funniest thing he did in his young life was to misspell "murder" on a grammar school quiz. "Murter" became his moniker. It tickled both sides of his funny bone. It was a mistake and it was macabre. In fact, if I ever wanted to make my son laugh, all I had to do was say "murter" and Dylan would go to pieces, practically peeing himself.

Chapter Four

After a while, during those early years of Dylan's existence, the evidence began to pile up. The signs started to point in an unavoidable direction, not so much for me, I could give a rat's ass what anyone thought of my son, but for Dylan himself.

The boy was starting to feel the pain. He was starting to realize that he was different.

It was becoming clear to everyone, himself included, that Dylan had problems picking up social cues, even the simplest of social cues. He laughed in the wrong places. He cried at the wrong times. Loud noises and group singing confused him, made him freak out, lose it big time. He couldn't go to other kids' birthday parties for fear they would start singing "Happy Birthday" at the top of their lungs, reducing him to violent tears.

He couldn't read people's expressions at all, not even the most basic expressions, those social cues that even infants can begin to sense six months into their lives. He had absolutely no clue what people thought about him or his behavior. Furthermore, he didn't appear to care, couldn't give a damn whether people liked him or not. He had no friends.

The fact was that he didn't really bother much with people at all. Dylan would just wander around by himself, in the backyard, in the laundry room downstairs, any place where he could live in his own fantasy world.

Only God knew what Dylan was thinking. Lettie and I certainly didn't.

Dylan would make strange noises and sounds, and it wasn't entirely clear whether he was even enjoying himself. The only thing that was totally clear, was that he was in constant motion, never standing still, never able to shut off the perpetual motion machine that was his body, that was his mind.

His mates at school were starting to make fun of him, starting to be cruel, as only little kids can be. They laughed at his noises. They mocked his outbursts. Dylan started having horrific emotional meltdowns whenever he was confronted with unexpected change. If I came home at an odd time, which I frequently did because I worked weird hours, Dylan would burst into tears and scream: "Go away, go away!!!"

At first, I thought my kid hated me, really hated me. I was devastated as any parent would be. Here I was a young parent and my only child couldn't stand me. It took me a while, but I eventually realized it wasn't me, that it had nothing to do with me. I suddenly realized that the kid hated change, any kind of unexpected change. I realized I needed to call ahead and give Dylan enough time to know when I would be arriving. Then, Dylan could adjust and deal with it. Then, he could plan.

And it worked. With proper notice, Dylan was a dream kid, the little kid who runs up to meet his daddy at the door, the little kid who jumps into his father's arms, just like something out of a sappy television ad.

But no matter what tricks I thought up to work around Dylan's discomfort and idiosyncrasies, it was becoming increasingly indisputable -- life was not going to be easy for the boy.

He was falling farther and farther behind with his grades. He was overwhelmed by his teacher and intimidated by his classmates. He was flailing. He was going to drown if something wasn't done soon.

In the end, even I was finally forced to admit it. They're right. The bastards. He's not an eccentric genius. There's something awry. He's not the same as other kids.

So Lettie and I took him to the specialists, the best we could find. It wasn't long before the verdict came back, loud and clear.

Dylan was autistic. High functioning. No doubt. Adorable, fascinating, extraordinarily fun to be with, absolutely. But autistic nonetheless.

Lettie and I were crushed, overwhelmed. We had no idea what to do next, how to handle this horrendous blindside from the fates.

And then one day when I didn't think it could get any worse, one day when Dylan was only six years old, he popped into my bedroom as I was getting dressed to go to work. He had the saddest eyes I had ever seen.

"What is it, Dylan?"

Daddy?" he asked, his voice confused and upset, searching for guidance, for answers.

"Yes, son?"

"Will my brain always be like this?"

A hostile, burning anger welled up inside my chest. My brain roared. Fuck you, God! Fuck you, Universe! Fuck you, whoever did this to my son! But my rage quickly melted away, unable to sustain itself, replaced by a total and abject sense of helplessness.

I wanted to die.

Chapter Five

They say that autistic people and animals see the world the way it really is, that the rest of us see the world the way we think it should be.

There was a study done some years back, where a bunch of people were asked to watch a video featuring basketball players passing a ball around.

The viewers were asked to count the number of times the basketball was passed between the players. It was pretty tricky to do because the players were running around like crazy and passing the ball faster and faster. It was almost impossible to keep up with them.

But a funny thing happened in this video, a funny thing that almost all "normal" people couldn't see, couldn't pick up on. A woman in a gorilla costume jumped in and out of the video while the basketball was being passed around.

Eighty percent of regular people, so-called "normal" people, never saw the woman in the gorilla suit. Their brains told them that it would be impossible for a woman in a gorilla suit to be in the middle of a basketball game.

Actually, it was the cortex, the most advanced and sophisticated part of their brains, that told them it was impossible. That's what cortexes do. They short-cut reality to help people reach conclusions faster. Sometimes this is just what we need. It's a survival instinct, really, developed back in prehistoric times. When we're in danger, we don't have time to think, we don't have time to deal with reality. When the lion, or the tiger, or the mastodon, is moving in, we just need to move as quickly as we can. That's when a fully functioning cortex can make the difference between life and death.

It is also turns out that the cortex is the part of the brain that has been damaged or underdeveloped in most autistic people.

So, when that same basketball video was shown to a bunch of autistic people, the video with the ball-passing players and the woman in the gorilla suit, they could spot her every time. One hundred percent of them saw what was really going on, precisely what was going on, not what the cortex in their brains told them was going on. They saw something the rest of us couldn't. They saw the truth.

Dylan's doctor explained the situation to me one time.

"Most of us have a mechanism inside us that helps us to concentrate. For example, right now, you are concentrating on what I am saying, but you can also hear the air conditioner going in the background, and see that fly buzzing around by the window over there, out of the corner of your eye.

"You choose to make what I am saying your main focus. That's a choice you make. And a choice that's pretty easy for you to make. But this is almost impossible for Dylan. The ability to focus on just one thing, the thing he wants to concentrate on, escapes him, does not come easily," the doctor continued calmly and in earnest.

"For him, he might be focusing on what I'm saying, right this second, but then he notices the air conditioning sound and switches his focus to that, and then he sees the fly and switches his focus to that, and so forth... just keeps noticing new things and getting distracted..."

For the first time, I got it, the full impact of it.

"Then he will never be able to drive a car," I said.

"Probably not," the doctor said, glumly, but quickly added, "But you never know. It just depends on how well he can learn to focus. We can give him medicine and coaching to see if that helps."

"And he'll never be able to hold down a job, support himself," I was shocked at the revelations that were suddenly coming at me like the punches of a mean-spirited prizefighter.

"Like I said, we'll just have to wait and see," the doctor said. "We'll just have to wait and see what happens with the behavioral therapy and the drugs."

Jesus Effing Christ.

I was overwhelmed, suffocating, choking on my own emotions.

Jesus Effing Christ.

A few months later, after treatment had begun, I remember going into Dylan's bedroom and looking down at my sleeping son, the latest in a long line of Bonner males, but the first ever with autism.

"Dylan, son, I know the doctors are playing pharmaceutical Russian roulette with your little brain, a brain that isn't even fully developed yet. I know the psychologists are dusting off every behavioral therapy gimmick they can get their hands on to try to crack the code that is your brain." I watched my offspring's chest go up and down with rhythmic breathing.

"It must be awful for you, being jerked around this way, by the drugs, by the therapy. It must be so confusing. I swear to God, son, if I could trade places with you, I'd do it in a heartbeat. But I can't. I can't even fucking do that.

"The big, fat, ugly truth of the matter is that your dad is completely and utterly powerless, useless, when it comes to your autism. I'm just no match. It's not even a fair fight.

"I am so sorry, son. I can't even begin to tell you how sorry I am."

I shut off Dylan's Dopey nightlight, walked out of my son's room, closing the door behind me.

Dylan was a bit of a savant and could reel off dates like he had a calendar in his brain, spouting out birthdays and anniversaries for everyone he'd ever met. And, more miraculously, you could throw out a date, say, April 19, in the following year, and he would announce, in an instance, without expression: "It's a Tuesday." And you know what? He was always right. You could look it up. He never got it wrong.

In fact, one time I got pulled over by the cops for doing 40 miles an hour in a 25 mile per hour zone. Lettie was in the front seat beside me. We were taking Dylan out to dinner for his eighth birthday.

The towering cop leaned into the driver's side window and delivered the classic line: "Do you know how fast you were going?"

Just as I was about to crank up the bullshit machine, a little voice from behind me piped up: "Forty-three."

I turned around slowly, with an expression of incredulity. Son, you are not being helpful here. The cop craned in to see where the voice had come from.

"On May 2, he went fifty-two," Dylan added.

I was flabbergasted. Lettie too.

“On February 21, he went thirty-eight,” Dylan continued on, expressionless.

“On March 11, he went forty-four.”

By this time, it was pretty clear Dylan was never going to stop. There was no malice in his voice, no overt attempt to put his father behind bars forever. He was simply responding to a question from a law enforcement official, someone he had been told repeatedly to respect.

“On January 30, he went twenty-nine…”

By this time, Lettie, me and, even the officer, were in tears, laughing so hard we couldn’t stop. We could barely catch our breath.

Only Dylan remained expressionless, and relentless.

"On March 9, he went..."

Finally, the policeman, tears running down his cheeks, intervened.

"That's fine, son," he wheezed. "I am not going to give your father a ticket." And then looking at me, the officer added, "But I am going to have to ask you to listen to that little voice in the backseat every once in a while and slow down."

It was at this particular point in time that Lettie and I, and even Dylan, realized that the lad had super human powers, that he was for all intents and purposes a flesh and bones, meat supercomputer, a human memory machine.

Forget that Dylan had saved my bacon and spared me a ticket, the boy had special skills, special powers that only he knew how to deploy.

One year, I entered Dylan in a Special Olympics for autistic kids. Dylan loved running so I signed him up for both the 100 and the 200 meter races. Dylan did not finish well in either event, but had a hell of a good time trying. His blond locks flapped in the spring breeze as he brought up the rear, all smiles and happiness.

For his third event -- Dylan was required to compete in three events under the rules of the Special Olympics – I picked standing long jump, largely because there was no one in line waiting to do that event.

After showing Dylan how to compete in the event with a few leaps of my own, I led him to the toe line for his jump. With barely a second's worth of preparation, Dylan swung his arms back and forth and leapt out into the grassy field in front of him.

"Oh my God!" screamed the girl behind the table. "He just shattered the Queens Borough record."

Dylan seemed truly unimpressed.

"Dylan," I yelled. "You broke the record. Way to go!"

Dylan remained nonplussed.

"Dylan," I added. "No one in Queens, no one in the history of Queens, has ever done that before, has ever jumped as far as you just did."

Dylan looked up at me matter-of-factly.

"Dad, Queens is not even a city. It's just part of a city. It's pretty small. Can I go for another run?"

The kid has no ego. He is just a purveyor of facts.

"Sure, son," I said, shaking my head. "Go for a run."

A year later, Dylan participated in the same Olympics. I was doing a rare gig upstate and called home to find out how my son had done.

"Did you run the 200 meters, Dylan?"

"Yes, father, I did," the boy said with his usual formality.

"Did you have fun?"

"Yes I did."

"Where did you finish?" I asked, wondering if he was dead last again.

“On the other side of the track, Dad,” Dylan said, his voice full of exasperation. It never occurred to him that his father might be asking where he had placed in the race.

Sometimes, I wondered if Dylan’s reality was not a much nicer place than mine, a world where materialism and rankings and false measuring sticks had no place at all.

Chapter Six

Open mikes are the lowest form of comedic endeavor. They are nothing short of torture. They are about as much fun as putting sharp toothpicks in your eyes. No one pays attention to your act except for maybe the friends you were able to bring along with you.

The good thing about doing open mikes is the chance it gives you to work on your routine.

The only other advantage to doing them is that you can tell friends and acquaintances, maybe even gorgeous girls you just happen to meet at your loser job at the grocery store, that you are, in fact, a stand-up comic. And that ain't necessarily a bad thing to have in your hip pocket.

But for a comedian just starting out, his primary job is to make sure that he can make it up the first rung of the comedy club ladder, get promoted from an open mike show to a "bringer" show, get promoted from private in the Army to private first class in the Army. The biggest difference between an open mike and a bringer is that an agent or a booker will invite you to a bringer. You can't just show up at them like you can for an open mike.

In either situation, your job is to bring in customers, plain and simple. Entertaining them once they get there is laudable, but not essential. Your job is to get them there in the first place, bums in seats, hooples who will pay for cover charges and two-drink minimums. That's what club owners want, that's all they're really interested in. They could give a shit if you're funny.

If you are funny, that's nice, that's a bonus. But your talent doesn't matter a damn if you don't bring your fans along with you.

For bringers, there is usually a booking agent who guarantees the club that he or she will fill the place up with comics and their friends. It's a good deal for the booker and a good deal for the club. The booking agent generally gets to keep the cover charges. The joint keeps all the booze and food revenue.

The comic, at least in the beginning, gets nothing, zilch, nada. You're working for free so that the other two groups – the agents and the clubs -- can feed their families. Your family will just have to wait until you're a star, or at least competent enough to not embarrass yourself or the club.

With no income coming in, the young comic is really working for his dream, a dream that he will be discovered, discovered tonight hopefully, and instantly be transported out of this dank and dreary dive of a club onto *Comedy Central* or *Saturday Night Live*, or at least, someplace where he can get paid real money, someplace where someone who didn't know him before tonight, will actually come out to see his show again because they actually want to see him perform.

That's the dream.

But do you know how many people have the same dream, how many people are busting their humps to get into comedy, how many people really think that they have a shot at the big time, how many people were told by somebody at some point in their lives, "Hey, you're really funny, you should think about becoming a comedian some day? Do you know how many of these people there are out there today? Millions, maybe even billions.

They are just like all the musicians and actors and authors and filmmakers and professional athletes, galaxies full of dreamers, universes full of pretenders, who actually believe that tonight will be the night.

They all dream that this time the applause will bring down the house, the crowd won't be able to stop laughing, even if it wanted to. Tonight will be the night when it all comes together, when the bathroom in this dive doesn't stink anymore, when the bouncer and the maître d' don't treat you like a scumbag anymore, when the representative from *The Tonight Show* comes hustling over to your table after the show to sign you to a multi-performance contract, the night when the girl of your dreams comes to your show and melts your heart away.

I stood in the downstairs kitchen of the Galabov's two-family house. Lettie and her dad were in the living room, having one of those patented father/daughter chats that define life, at least family life. I knew what I was doing was wrong, but I couldn't help but listen in.

"Is he really the one for you, darling?" her father was asking. "He's a comedian, honey. Is that what you really want, a clown for a husband?"

"Daddy," Lettie snapped back, "He is not a clown. He is an artist, a very funny person and the man I love."

"I know, sweetheart," her father said, softening his tone and demeanor. "But will he be able to support you in a way you want to be supported, the way you deserve to be supported?"

"Daddy, I don't need anyone to support me. I have a great job as creative director at Johnson & Kravitz, and a bright future ahead of me. If Lance and I decide to get married, we will get married for love, not for what we can do for each other financially."

I loved my fiancée to pieces, even if her argument hinged largely on the premise that because she was doing so well at work, she could afford to be in love with a loser like me. Sock it to your old man, baby. Sock it to him.

Rather than waiting for my future father-in-law to come up with another painful zinger, I decided to head out into the backyard and contemplate the beauty of the day, and the magic of having someone who loved me, someone who was firmly in my corner.

Lettie was one of three daughters in the Galabov clan, the youngest and by all accounts, the smartest. She had graduated from Brown at the tender age of 19, majoring in marketing. She was a natural, born to succeed in the business of making ads for television.

She had always been the apple of her daddy's eye. He tried to spoil her rotten, but she would have none of it. She refused special treatment as the baby of the family, demanded that she be meted out the same punishment or rewards as her sisters for committing commensurate crimes or achieving similar successes.

It's not that she believed in equality. She knew she was different, that she was exceptional in many ways. But she also knew she had her faults, impatience and intolerance being the most obvious. She had a tough time waiting for others to catch up with her lightning quick ideas and she did not suffer fools gladly. Having said this, Lettie firmly believed that everyone has special talents. They just need to spend their lives trying to figure out what they are and how to use them for good.

Born with an abundance of natural beauty and cunning charm, she knew her real attribute was her fierce sense of independence, her almost biological need to succeed, to achieve whatever she needed, or for that matter, wanted.

"When I set my sights on something," she once confided to a girlfriend during an overnight grammar school sleepover, "I don't give up until I get it."

She told me that when she stumbled on me at *Trader Joe's,* she knew in an instant she had to have me. To my chagrin, she couldn't explain exactly she why was attracted to me. But she did say there was something about my bumbling, self-effacing attempt at humor coupled with my boyish innocence and rumpled clothes that appealed to her. I was cute, she said, and needed looking after. In other words, I was a project, and one she was eager to undertake. Not exactly what I wanted to hear, but when you're in my position, a grocery store manager-cum-broke comic, you take what you can get.

Lettie said she never regretted her decision. She was not the goo-goo, ga-ga type. (I was. She wasn't.). But she said our life together was simple. It was pure. It was just what she wanted. And even with all the trials and tribulations that Dylan brought, Lettie loved our family, loved the way all the different pieces fit together into one, unbreakable whole.

God, she was something. God, do I miss her.

Chapter Seven

Not that any amount of money could ever compensate for Lettie's death, but the money Dylan and I got from the insurance company helped us set Dylan up in a nice school for autistic kids, a school that wasn't too expensive but more than I would have been able to afford on a day manager's salary, even at an upscale grocery store like *Trader Joe's.*

We could have bought a new house with the money, but we decided to stay in Astoria, Queens. I was obsessed with finding a way to guarantee that Dylan could eventually support himself in the event I died as well. So, that meant school.

Once Dylan was ensconced, the school administrators put him through all kinds of tests to determine what he had an aptitude for, as well as finding out what he actually wanted to do with his life.

The only real interest Dylan had shown was to hang out with me and the other comedians, but I didn't see a real future for him as a comic. There didn't appear to be a huge demand for "murter" and "Abraham Lincoln" jokes.

The teachers at the new school were amazing and they really put a lot of effort into finding out what Dylan would be good at, but they only came up with dry wells.

Finding a place in the world for my son, finding a place that he could call his own, was going to be a lot more difficult than I thought it would be.

Some people ask me why my parents and Lettie's parents don't take on a more active role in Dylan's upbringing. I have some theories.

The truth is autistic grandchildren confuse grandparents. They don't know what to do with them.

A lot of people spend their whole lives waiting to be grandparents and they have this vision in their heads about what it's going to be like when the day arrives. When the day finally arrives and they finally get a grandchild, they start going to town, fulfilling their fantasy, buying the kid all kinds of toys and stuff, generally doing all the things they had dreamed about doing for their grandkids.

Then, it turns out, that the kid doesn't play with toys, doesn't get into dolls or trucks, doesn't understand them. And he or she doesn't hug or snuggle either, and do all the other things that the grandparents have been waiting for all those years.

A kind of weirdness sets in. The parents of the autistic child keep trying to explain to their parents, the new grandparents, what's going on. But it's not an easy message to convey because a lot of times the parents themselves are having a tough time accepting that their child is not "normal," not exactly turning out the way their dreams had planned it either.

After a while, after all the tests and the examinations, after all of the medical visits and verdicts, when it's become clear that this child is autistic, that he or she is not just going through a phase, that this is something that is going to have to be dealt with for an entire lifetime, a lot of grandparents just kind of fry, kind of move off to one side, turn the whole kit and caboodle back over to the parents.

It's not like they disappear, at least not entirely. It's just that they back way off from how they were behaving when the child was first born.

I think maybe it's because no one, on either side of a family, wants to admit that maybe it was the chromosomes or DNA in their blood that caused the problem. Maybe it's just easier if the grandparents take a backseat and let their children handle this issue on their own.

To be fair, as the years go by, the grandparents will throw in their encouragements from time to time. "He seems to be doing so much better. It's almost like night and day."

I bite my tongue but always feel like saying: "Of course he's going to seem better if you only see him once every six months. He's not a freak. He has a disability. Other than that, he's just like any other kid. They grow. They change. That's why they're called kids."

But in the end, I realize the world's a hard enough place to live in without any of us casting judgment. We all have our share of problems, big problems. Nobody gets through the gauntlet of life without them.

And of course, it would be hard for Lettie's folks to look at either Dylan or me without remembering their dear, sweet daughter.

They say that losing a child is the worst thing that can ever happen to anyone. They say that no one should ever survive their child.

I cannot imagine the pain and agony involved. If losing your child is worse than losing your soul mate, your partner, the love of your life, then it has to be worse than death. It has to the worst punishment God can inflict on anyone.

That's why I didn't give my in-laws too hard a time. That's why I left them alone.

They have suffered enough.

Chapter Eight

Over the past 20 years, scientists have figured out something comics never will – that laughter actually has very little to do with humor.

Recent research shows that the brain has ancient wiring which ignites laughter. It is used primarily to help teach the young how to play with one another. Laughter stimulates euphoria circuits in young brains and allows them to convince other youngsters that they want to play, not fight.

Humans start laughing at about four months of age. By one, they are into tickling, and from there they quickly advance to cartoons and joke telling. But the really fascinating part of the study is the disconnect between the sophistication of a joke and why people actually laugh or don't laugh at it. It turns out, there is no connection at all between the two.

Here's an example.

Scientists have been testing this really bad joke on folks for years:

"Two muffins are baking in the oven.

One of them yells, 'Wow, it's hot in here!'

And the other one replies: 'Holy cow! A talking muffin!'"

Is that funny or not? Apparently, it doesn't really matter, one way or the other.

What the research shows is that you should be able to predict whether you're going to laugh at it or not, depending on a number of pre-determined criteria that have absolutely nothing to do with the joke itself.

For example, women laugh at that joke more than men. Women like to be part of a larger group. Laughter is a way for them to show they're inclusive. If someone who is your boss or your teacher tells that joke you will be more likely to laugh at it than if a peer or a subordinate tells it. Brown-nosing, social climbing and gaining recognition turn out to be powerful motives for laughter.

Why? Because laughter is a survival tool, a social instrument for communicating your status and willingness to submit to someone else, a way for you to show that you are non-threatening, a way for you to show that you want to be accepted.

That's what the scientists found out.

Laughter is not about getting a joke. It's about getting along with other people.

So maybe that's why comedy clubs are set up the way they are. The comic stands on a small stage, slightly higher than his audience, up in front of the room, like a professor or a boss at a company meeting.

And maybe, that's why many comics prefer a female audience. Women are always more relationship-oriented than men. They tend to laugh more than men, even if the jokes aren't all that funny. They're just trying to be polite.

The biggest mistake that folks make when they start out in stand-up comedy is to think that they should learn to improvise, think on their feet, just make stuff up, witty stuff, and throw it into their routines.

But the truth is that stand-up is much more like acting than improv. Some people can do both – stand-up and improv, but they are very rare.

Improv people are witty, quick on their feet. They're allowed to make mistakes because eventually they're going to come up with something really clever, really funny. The audience knows that and cuts them a break.

Comics are perfectionists, tacticians. If you want to be a comic, practice, practice, practice. Don't make shit up while you're performing. Use the material you've already written. Work on your delivery. Work on your timing. But know your lines cold. The secret is to make the audience think you are improvising when you're actually delivering your bit just the way you planned it.

I know that when the lights go up, I have to make the audience believe that this is the very first time that I've ever told that joke, convince them that this particular joke cracks my ass up, that I can't even believe how funny it really is.

And I have to do this, even though I am sick to death of telling the same dumb joke, over and over and over. But that's the job.

If you don’t like it, do something else. Like, improv, maybe.

From the time I stepped out onto the stage, I knew from experience that I only had about eight seconds to win my audience over. After that, they pretty much made up their minds what they thought of me. And it was no use trying to dissuade them.

I learned this the hard way.

At first, I would try to dress up like all the other comics, in a black shirt, with a black tee-shirt underneath, a pair of wrinkled blue jeans, and some cool “I could really give a shit” shoes. I thought I looked pretty good. But the audiences didn’t. They thought I looked like a 34-year-old loser who was trying to look like all the other comedians who were in their mid-to-late 20s. When I finally figured it out, things started to perk up for my act. I started showing up in brightly-colored Benetton sweaters, khaki pants, dock-siders, and blue buttoned down shirts, in other words, like some overgrown preppie. It worked like a charm.

I began making a point of how different I looked from all the other comics. I would frequently open my act by finding a cute young blonde in the front row, and mimic what I thought she might be thinking. *"Hey,"* I would say, looking right at her, *"I know what you're thinking. You're thinking that guy looks just like my older brother's best friend."*

And everyone in the room would look at me, and think, yeah, he does sort of look like my older brother's best friend. I knew that confirming people's prejudices, getting them to believe that what they see is the truth, is a huge part of comedy, maybe even the biggest part.

Tuesday night, small crowd, dingy ass bar.

"Yeah, I do triathlons," I started, looking all the world like a scrawny bean pole of a specimen who could barely do a sit-up, much less a pull-up. *"I did the New York Olympic Triathlon just last week."*

I paused to get my timing right, to make sure I had my rhythm down.

"I did the whole thing, ran six miles around Central Park, biked 24 miles up to Westchester, and then the hardest part, I swam a mile in the Hudson.

"Some people say to me... 'Lance... Why was that the hardest part?'

"You ever try to keep a joint lit while you're swimming?

It was a good night. The audience was paying attention. Not killing themselves with laughter, but enjoying themselves and showing their appreciation.

"People say to me.... Lance.... So what was it like to swim in the Hudson River?

"Tastes like chicken... only different."

Another round of solid laughs.

"I bought myself one of those Wii Fi exercise gadgets the other day. Have you seen those things...? Have you played with one of those yet?" I barged ahead.

"They're amazing. You just stand on top of them and they can tell you what your real age is... not your chronological age... but your real age. Like, do you have the body of a 20-year-old... a

40-year-old... or a 60-year-old...?

Pause.

"In my case, it wouldn't even give me a number... It just told me to lie down... immediately!"

There are basically two kinds of comedians – comedians who like their audiences and comedians who hate their audiences. I am sure there are more of the latter than the former.

I fall into the first camp. I love audiences. But I have to admit it is hard sometimes not to get pissed off at some of the folks sitting right in front of me. Every performance, me and all the other comics in the line-up put our hearts and souls into our work, put our ideas and thoughts out there for public inspection, and frequently, ridicule.

In a comedy club, there are a million forms of abuse. Some dude who thinks he's funny will start giving you shit while you're on stage, or start talking to his girlfriend while you're performing, or knock over his drink in a loud, drunken display of self-absorption.

When these things happen to me, I feel like screaming: "Do you have any fucking idea how hard this is, any idea how much work I put into this act?" It is not a profession for the faint of heart. That is for sure. Thinking up a joke, writing it down, learning how to deliver it, slaving to get the timing perfect, and then actually getting out there, and trying to make a room full of slightly, or totally, inebriated strangers laugh, these are not easy things to do.

But as painful as heckling, intentional or unintentional, can be, silence is actually the most painful form of disapproval, by far. It is agonizing, a dark sea of bored eyes, not a smile in sight.

Brutal. So I would rather have some form of acknowledgement, even if it is a bit obnoxious.

I remember one night, in the middle of my routine, when I was having a particularly tough time of it, a drunken woman suddenly interrupted, saying that she wanted to help me out. Slurring her words, she said she would take a dump on the top of her table if the audience would start laughing at me. I couldn't believe my ears. This was her way of trying to help? Imagine what she would have offered if she were trying to heckle me? But God bless her. At least, she was in my corner.

I know that the really great comedians always find a way to hold it together, come what may. To them, the audience is always right. If the folks in the room don't think a joke is funny, it isn't funny, no matter how much effort went into it.

I can't argue with them. Humor is in the eye of the beholder. But sometimes, I just wish people would consider the possibility

that a $10 cover charge and a two-drink minimum doesn’t give
them free rein to piss all over somebody’s dream.

Chapter Nine

"We will discuss this in the car on the ride back."

"NO, we won't!"

Dylan had never talked back to me before. This was a new, and potentially serious, development.

"I SAID we will talk about this in the car on the way home."

"NO, we won't," Dylan repeated.

I couldn't believe my ears. Dylan giving me lip, and in public.

We were standing in a crowded ice cream parlor, a favorite summer haunt packed to the rafters with sun-burnt holiday makers. Dylan, Lettie and I had come with another family, in two carloads full of kids and adults. Our two families were sharing a multi-story vacation rental and had decided it would be a treat to go get some ice cream after a super-hot day at the beach.

Everything had been going well until Dylan's outburst. Now, everyone was turning around to see what the father-son confrontation was all about.

"Dylan," I said as firmly as I could. "Don't make me say it again." And then of course, as parents do, I said it again: "We WILL talk about it on the car ride home."

"NO we won't," Dylan repeated.

I lost it. I was furious. I would never hit a kid, but I was doing all I could not to yank Dylan's arm out of its socket.

The whole incident started because one of the foreign interns behind the counter had not done a particularly brilliant job of securing the one scoop of pistachio ice cream that was perched in Dylan's sugar cone. As a result, it toppled out of the cone and into his hand. That's when Dylan started screaming.

"That guy doesn't know what he's doing," Dylan said loud enough for the whole room to hear. "He talks funny too."

I was appalled, and more than a little embarrassed.

"Dylan, give me the ice cream and stop making a scene."

"He doesn't know what he's doing and he talks funny too," Dylan was adamant.

"Please stop saying that. We WILL talk about it in the car on the ride home."

"NO, we won't!"

I was standing in front of a roomful of shocked ice cream eaters who were waiting to see if I was going to let my parental authority be challenged so publicly by this little brat.

"We WILL talk about it in the car on the ride home," I repeated even louder than before.

"NO, we won't!"

Dylan and I had reached the ultimate stand-off. It was a very uncomfortable situation, for everyone in the shop, not just the two of us.

My eyes blazing, I grabbed ahold of Dylan's arm and started to march out the door.

But that's when Dylan blurted out: "You and I can't discuss it in the car ride home. We came in DIFFERENT cars."

I stopped for a second, looked down at Dylan and then belted out a hearty laugh. So we did, son. So we did. We came in different cars.

I released my grip on Dylan's arm and gently took my son by the hand. Then, we strolled out of the ice cream stand, ignoring all the gaping customers who were still trying to digest what they had just witnessed.

I knew Dylan was different, but frankly, I didn't care. To the contrary, I actually reveled in it.

Sometimes I would take a look at Dylan, and think that the boy belonged in an Abercrombie & Fitch ad. He was that good looking, Beach Boy blonde hair, piercing blue eyes, long and lean, almost always tanned, a feast for a young girl's eyes.

But Dylan was oblivious. He couldn't care less.

It was not that he was disinterested in girls, biologically disinterested in them, it was more like he was disinterested in being interested, if that makes any sense. In other words, he'd just preferred to think about other things for the time being, like memorizing all the weather patterns around the world, figuring out the birthplaces of all the U.S. Presidents, compiling a cranial database of license plate and telephone numbers.

What did he do with all that information? Did he really need to know what the highs and lows were today in Kuala Lumpur?

Who made the decisions in that little brain of his about what to hold onto and what to let go of?

I wish I knew. I wished with all my might that I could crawl inside that beautiful head, just for an hour, just for a day, and find out what was going on in there, what it was like to be autistic, what it was like to be Dylan.

Chapter Ten

The whole thing started when one of my friends, Donnelly, a big Irish-American kid from what was left of Hell's Kitchen, dared me to do stand-up comedy. We were having a couple of drinks and the conversation came around to what were some of the hardest things to do in life.

We had gotten through the usual suspects after a couple of beers -- public speaking, asking a girl to marry you, hitting a baseball, etc. -- when Donnelly said, "I can't imagine anything being harder than doing stand-up comedy."

Donnelly, who worked with me down at *Trader Joe*'s, insisted that standing under blaring lights, in a cheesy nightclub, trying to make semi-drunk, or totally drunk, strangers laugh their asses off was as tough a job as there was.

I was three beers into the night. Emboldened, I decided to take

Donnelly on.

"Oh, I don't think that it would be all that hard," I said brazenly.

"You don't, do you?" asked Donnelly. "Fifty bucks says you can't do it."

"Oh yeah."

"Oh yeah," said Donnelly. "Fifty bucks says you're chicken."

"Oh, yeah," I repeated.

"Oh yeah," Donnelly countered.

"Okay," I said, taking another swig of beer. "You're on. I'll do it."

And that's how it started. That's how I got into the comedy game, exactly one week before I met Lettie, exactly one week before I told her that I was a comic while we were standing at the organic spinach stand, while I was trying to chat her up and score points.

I did it, humiliated myself, but did it. Won my fifty bucks.

It was the longest 10 minutes of my life. Standing up there, under the lights, with the scratchy microphone, trying to tell jokes while everyone in the audience was talking loudly, clinking their glasses, swilling down their booze, and generally ignoring me. All except for Donnelly and the gang, who were all laughing at me, not with me, not at my jokes, but at me.

"I read in the paper the other day that 60 percent of Americans are living from paycheck to paycheck," I blurted out nervously, trying to be heard over the din. *"I couldn't believe it. I called up my agent and asked him, 'Hey, what the hell is a paycheck?'"*

I thought this was going to be a hilarious joke, a joke that would bring the house down. But nobody laughed. No one was paying attention. My alleged pals weren't much help either. They just grinned up at me from out in the darkness, like I was a double-headed freak at a county fair.

It got worse. Much worse. Too painful to describe. But somehow I got through my maiden gig and stumbled off the stage.

Donnelly came over to give me some shit.

"Don't you say a fucking thing," I hissed angrily. "Go get me a drink and then hand over the fifty bucks."

A week later after I met Lettie, after I had done the open mike set and won $50 off Donnelly, I quickly signed up for lessons from some guy who claimed to have written jokes for Jerry Seinfeld's popular television show. I had to learn this comedy stuff and learn it fast. I couldn't afford to lose this girl and I had told her I was a comic, a real live comic, not a guy who does open mike sessions to win some bet he made when he was drunk. It cost me half my paycheck to sign up for this guy's comedy school, but it had to be done. She was that attractive, that alluring.

I had no idea, at the time that every comedy teacher in New York City claims to have written for Jerry Seinfeld. I also had no idea that the business plan for these comedy college profs was to teach a person the basics about telling jokes, listen to their students' abysmal attempts to tell the lousy ones they had written, schedule a performance where the comic-wannabes could invite all their friends and families, and then take a fairly sizeable chunk of the losers' money for providing all of those services, none of which were actually designed to get them job any time soon as actual comedians.

When I started in the biz, there were about three or four of these kind of schools in New York. There are more now, a lot more. As far as I can tell, everybody on the planet wants to be a comedian these days. I was still trying to figure out if I was one.

I have to admit my teacher really was a funny guy, had a pretty good teaching style. But truth be told, his class was a circus, a total, free-wheeling, crazy people-invited circus.

They were maybe one or two marginally funny people in the room, which was in a smallish venue, on the seventeenth floor of an old, worn-out, thread-bare New York hotel. And I wasn't one of them, one of the truly funny ones.

No, I fell into the second category, nice people who had been told by friends at some point in their lives that they were “funny” and that they should think about becoming comedians. These, by the way, are the same kind of people who tell you that you are so interesting that you should write a book.

The overwhelming majority of the would-be comics in the class didn’t fall into the funny category or even the friends who think you are funny category. These people, the third category, the largest category, are people who belong in jails or mental hospitals.

These people are not only not funny, they are downright scary. It is hard to figure out how some of them even came up with the $400 needed to take the course. Probably robbed somebody on the way to class.

Which brings up a very important point, a point that occurs to me all the time. Basically, all comics are crazy. Seriously. All of them.

Woody Allen was hilarious until everyone found out that he was dumping his movie star wife for his adopted daughter. Jonathan Winters spent his entire life going in and out of looney bins. Richard Pryor, who I thought might have been the funniest guy who ever lived, set himself ablaze with his crack pipe.

So, there I was in comedy class, hoping I could learn to be funny enough to win Lettie's heart and keep her from finding out that I was just a glorified broom boy at her favorite super market. The process was excruciatingly painful.

I will never forget that first night, the night I stood up in front of class, a full-fledged member in The Land of Misfit Toys.

I couldn't believe it. I stood there and plowed through all the jokes I had written during the week, and some of the ones I had used on open mike night. I thought they were pretty good, at least I did when I wrote them. But no one laughed. Not a soul. Not a one. Except for the professor who chuckled a couple of times. But hell, I was paying him. Of course, he was going to laugh.

At that point, I didn't realize that comedians, aside from being crazy, are also the single worst audiences in the world, at least when one of the other comics is performing.

They're all busy trying to remember their own jokes, all sweating their turn at the mike, all nervous wrecks on their way to the executioner. The last thing they are going to do is laugh at your jokes. To be fair, most of the time, they don't even hear them. And even if they do hear them, you are the competition. They wouldn't laugh at you if you were the funniest guy on earth.

I was feeling really sick up there in front of the class, like throw-up sick. I was feeling like maybe I should pack the whole thing in, feeling like I should just admit to Lettie that I was not really a comedian, that I was a fraud.

But a few minutes later, after I sat down, I felt a whole lot better. The guy right after me was terrible, even worse than me. He was so bad that he made me look like a modern day Bob Hope.

"I can tell my girlfriend's putting on some weight because I can't hear the stereo when she's sitting on my face," the comic said.

God, his stuff was bad, and old, too. I had heard that joke in seventh grade.

The teacher tried to explain to the guy that stealing somebody else's joke violated long-held comedic tradition. It happens all the time, but everybody knows that you're not supposed to do it. And if you get caught doing it, you're supposed to fess up right away. It's kind of like The Comic's Honor Code.

The comedic criminal at the microphone, a towering hulk of a man, unshaven and unkempt, wasn't taking the criticism very well.

"You saying that I stole that joke?" he said menacingly, his voice rising in anger, "Cuz I don't think I can just stand up here and let you get away with accusing me of stealing somebody else's joke."

The professor was looking around for help, looking around for somebody to pipe up and say: "C'mon, man. Everybody's heard that joke before. I heard it for the first time when I was in diapers."

But nobody did, no one bailed the professor out.

Eventually, the teacher apologized, said he might have gotten it wrong, that it probably was an original joke, and a damn good one at that.

Somehow, me and the others muddled through the five classes, got our diplomas, and went on to do our arranged, big gig at a famous New York comedy club. That was really what all of us would-be comics had paid the $400 for, to be able to tell somebody someday that we had played the Gotham Comedy Club, somebody, say, like a beautiful girl we had met in the grocery store where we worked.

What we would never tell anybody is that this show at the famous Gotham Comedy Club was at 5 p.m. on a Saturday, in the middle of the afternoon, when nobody was in the club except for the comedians themselves and the friends they had invited to come see them perform.

I was lucky. Practically, everybody from *Trader Joe's* showed up to see me. It was actually pretty great, really nice of them. They practically filled up the joint.

The angry comic, the one who stole the old joke, did not have anybody show up for him, didn't have anyone show up to hear him perform, not even a mother or a brother or anything. I actually felt kind of sorry for him. He was an asshole, no doubt, but he was also a human too.

My routine was passable. To be honest, I was kind of nervous, the lighting was off a bit and the mike was sort of static-y. But my material wasn't half bad, my timing wasn't totally klutzy and there were a bunch of hearty laughs from my entourage. All in all, I had made it through the gauntlet relatively unscathed.

But what I didn't know was that one of my friends, Donnelly, actually, the guy who had bet me fifty bucks to do the open mike gig, recorded the whole thing, warts and all, with his iPhone.

Before I even got home from the club, it was up on YouTube. And Donnelly sent out Facebook and Twitter updates with links to the video to about 500 people, who then passed it along to 500 more people. It was all over the place.

It was my very first real comedic performance, not an open mike, and it was not exactly the kind of performance that I wanted broadcast to the whole world, which, of course, is exactly why Donnelly had done it, to get back at me for winning the money.

But a funny thing happened to me. During the performance, while I was doing my shtick, I fell in love with comedy. It wasn't just a bet anymore. It was a passion. After that afternoon's performance, it was all I could think about, day and night, getting up and doing another gig. I had the bug. The problem was I didn't know if I was ever going to get another opportunity to play another club. I certainly didn't want to do any more open mikes.

Then, about a month later, out of the blue, I got a phone call from somebody named Mona. She claimed to be the daughter of a famous Jewish comedian. She also claimed that she wanted to be my agent.

"I need you to work the The Big Apple Comedy Club on Saturday night, the 8 p.m. show," she said.

She talked a mile a minute. "We usually only put on comedians who have been on television before," she lied. "But I think you've got talent, so I'm willing to give you a slot in the show."

I was stunned.

"How did you find me?" I asked, incredulous.

"I have a bunch of assistants who run around the Internet looking for comedic talent. They found you on YouTube. They told me you had a lot of interesting bits. I watched you. I thought you sounded pretty funny. I thought I would give you a call to see if we could work together."

It suddenly dawned on me that this was an elaborate prank, probably put on by the guys down at work, probably led by Donnelly. They had found this chick and were getting her to take the piss out of me, play a practical joke on me.

I decided to go along with the gag for a while.

"Sure," I said. "I'd be happy to make the scene. What should I wear?"

"Wear?" she said, puzzled. "Whatever you want."

There was an awkward pause.

Then she was back to speed rapping.

"So you're going to be there, right? Saturday night, 8 p.m.? The Big Apple Comedy Club? Lower Eastside. I can count on you. Right?"

"S-u-r-e," I said, dragging out the word.

"And you can bring some friends, right? A lot of friends, right? Like you did in the YouTube video show, right?"

"S—u—r--e," I said again, dragging the word out even longer this time.

Mona paused. She was trying to figure out if I had a speech impediment or something.

"Okay, then," she said, "Saturday night it is. Should be fun. See you then."

"Yeah, right," I said, quickly adding: "See you Saturday night."

And then, after a pause of my own, I threw in: "And tell Donnelly to shove it up his ass."

I was getting ready to hang up and have a good laugh, when Mona said, "Huh? What the fuck are you talking about, dude? You're going to be there with friends on Saturday night, right? I can count on you, right?

"I don't know from Donnelly," she said, dryly. "But you'd better be there on time, and you'd better be there with all your friends. This is your big chance. Don't blow it."

Wait a second. This wasn't a put-on. She really was a famous comedian's daughter. I really did have an agent now. I couldn't believe it.

I started back-peddling like crazy. "Yeah, sure, I'll be there, with bells on, with lots of friends, lots and lots of friends."

Hey, Lettie, I thought. Take a look at me now. I really am a professional comic.

Chapter Eleven

"You weren't bad," she said with a smile. "You were good, actually. You were really good."

No I wasn't, I thought. It was my third night working for Mona and I was still very green. But who gave a shit? Lettie was here and she was talking to me, actually talking to me. We hadn't had much time to talk after my original gig at the Gotham Club.

"Want to go get something to eat?" I asked.

"Aren't you supposed to stay and watch the other comedians?"

"Yeah, I meant after the show."

"Won't that be about 10 p.m.?"

"Oh yeah, what time is it now? 9:30?"

She was right. It was getting late. I got so wound up for these gigs that I would forget what time it was. I had been in the number seven slot (which really stinks) and there were two more comics to go, each with a 10-minute routine, each of them straining to get a little extra time in before they got pulled off the stage. It was going to be a while.

"Well, can you stay?" I pleaded.

She hesitated, then relented: "Sure. I can stay."

So she stayed, and we sat in the dark, and listened to bad comedy, really bad comedy. On this particular night, the last two comics had made a fatal error in judgment. They had kept drinking while the other performers were on stage. Since they were the last two standing, they were pretty wasted when they got up there. And nothing is worse on your timing than being drunk and playing to an audience that has comedy-fatigue from watching so many other comics before you, an audience that is more than a little bit in the bag themselves.

But it didn't matter to me. It didn't matter that the comedians sucked, or that the club sucked. All the clubs pretty much sucked, even the allegedly high end ones in New York, Chicago and Los Angeles. They were all holes in the ground, cheap spaces made to look pretty, just pretty enough to make their owners money.

It didn't even matter that Lettie wasn't talking to me, or holding my hand, or making eye contact with me. She couldn't. The performers were performing, and she was way too polite to do anything that might distract them.

What mattered to me was that she was sitting next to me; that she hadn't left, that I was in with a chance. That's all that mattered.

Chapter Twelve

The truth of the matter is that Margie isn't really fooling anyone. She doesn't look like a girl. She has hands the size of snow shovels and a fake, phony falsetto voice that sounds like a big man trying to talk like a little girl, actually, more like an old guy making fun of a little girl.

She has a head the size of a prize-winning County Fair pumpkin and eyes to match, big, giant owl eyes that kind of bulged out like a pair of golf balls half buried in the sand. And no woman ever had a nose like that, a nose that looked like it belonged on a light heavyweight pugilist, all bent and swollen looking.

Maybe, all of this is true because, until three years ago, Margie actually was a guy, and not just any guy, but a large, lumbering, Lenny "Of Mice and Men" type of a guy, a guy who decided that he must have been miscast and should really be a dame. That's what Marge used to call women back in the day, dames. That might have been an early indication that he was not fully ready to be integrated into the female population.

But it was his gender that Margie had been interested in changing, not his attitude. So he went through with the sex change operation and the hormone injections and all the other miserable stuff that one has to go through to switch to the opposite sex, and presto, magic-o, there he was, a woman. At least that's what he thought. To a lot of other people, he was more like a man dressed up as a woman, and not doing a very good job at that.

But rather than hide his light under a bushel basket, rather than wallow in the failure of an ill-advised gender swap, good ol' Margie -- actually the new, improved Margie – threw herself into her new identity with unbridled enthusiasm. She decided to take her show on the road. She became a stand-up comic.

Margie was one of the first comediennes, I had ever met. I saw her at the fourth show I did for Mona in a tiny, little backroom in a bar in Greenwich Village. Frankly as comics go, Margie was not very good. At least I didn't think so. The only funny thing about her was the way she looked, like a hairy cartoon gorilla in a Minnie Pearl outfit.

But for some inexplicable reason, I took to Margie, really liked spending time with her. Eventually, months after we first met, I introduced her to Dylan.

As I've pointed out, as a comedian Margie had her limits. But as a minder of children, as a caretaker for Dylan, she was the best, the absolute best. Maybe it was because they – Margie and Dylan -- were both so different from other people, both so unique, both struggling to find their place in this strange world, that their devotion to one another had no bounds.

They just loved hanging out together.

So, on those days when Lettie was at her agency thinking great thoughts and doing great things for her growing list of clients, and I was working in the produce section at *Trader Joe's*, pushing the broom and rearranging the vegetables, Margie would look after Dylan, taking him to the park, going on long walks, practicing her lame ass routines on him.

The kid loved every second of it.

At nights, Lettie would take over again, and Margie and I would head off to the comedy club du jour to ply our trade.

"Do you think that hearing really bad transgender comedy routines every day will warp him over time?" I would ask Lettie.

"Don't be ridiculous, honey," she'd say. "They are so good together.

"Margie just has a way of soothing him, giving him confidence that everything is going to be alright," Lettie continued. "I think he actually likes that sing-song falsetto of hers."

She never thought about Margie's sex change operation, while I thought about it all the time, probably because 90 percent of Margie's shtick was about her old gender versus her new gender.

As far as Lettie was concerned, if Margie thought she was a woman, then she was a woman. That's just the way Lettie was. She didn't accept people the way they were. She did one better. She accepted people the way they wanted to be accepted.

It was pretty mind-bending actually, the way Lettie was.

It could be really tough going in the early days.

I recalled a particularly awful night when there were only four people in the audience. It was a Tuesday and I was playing in some back room at a spare ribs joint in midtown. I had taken the slot at the last second, as a favor to Danny, a booker friend of mine, and boy, did it prove to be a mistake.

The place was a dive with a capital "D." One of the four people who came to the show was Donnelly, who was showing up to most of my gigs in those days. One of the other attendees was some super fat guy who looked like Jabba the Hutt with slimy tadpoles falling out of his mouth. He was only there, apparently, so that he could dig into a full rack of sauce-dripping ribs. And then there were two others, two tourists from France, who barely spoke English. Talk about a bad room, talk about a tough audience.

I stood behind the curtains in the back watching the first couple of comics die as they played to the near empty cafe. I couldn't look at the audience because all four attendees, including Donnelly, had zombie-like, vacant stares in their eyes, like they had been lobotomized or something.

I consoled myself by remembering that there were nine other comics who were going to have to play to the same pathetic crowd. And of course, that was based on the rather dubious and optimistic assumption that none of the four attendees was going to bolt early. I was sure the non-English speaking couple, who were almost all the way through their meal, were now wondering why they had ever let that hawker out on Eighth Avenue convince them to come to an American comedy show that they could barely understand.

The hawker outside who had corralled them was actually Guillermo, one of the comics on the card that night. That is one of the true indignities in my line of work, when the booker asks you to go out on the street and pass out three by five post cards that showcase the comedy club in general and tonight's performance in particular. It only happens when attendance for a show is so horrible that there is no choice but to beg passersby to come in and see the comedy. It can be more than a little humiliating, especially later on in the show, when you hear someone out in the audience, say to his friend, "Isn't that the guy who was passing out post cards in front of this place earlier tonight?"

I was in the number five slot tonight, and kept praying that some more people would come in and fill up the joint. I watched the first four comics struggle to find their rhythm, to keep their timing together in the face of no laughs other than Donnelly's polite chortle. And Donnelly was having a hard time making his laugh sound spontaneous since he had heard most of these routines a bunch of times before.

I was literally begging the heavens to send some new blood into the room to give me somebody to perform for, give me somebody with a frigging pulse, when a bunch of my other pals showed up. My prayers were answered.

As the fourth comic was winding up his bit, eight guys and a couple of girls from *Trader Joe's* arrived en masse to see me perform. There wasn't a sober one in the crowd. They had been drinking hard all night.

"Woo hoo," one of the girls screamed, as I took the stage. "Lance!!!!"

The French couple got up and left. I was convinced that Jabba would split too, but he wasn't going anywhere until he finished up his molten chocolate volcano cake, which was smothered in whipped cream and vanilla ice cream. I figured the dessert was part of the meal package the guy had paid for. Twelve hundred sixty-five calories and some lame comedy. What a deal.

I had to admit that when the kids from my workplace had come in, it was nice to finally have some support in the room. But it was definitely strange. There was Donnelly and Jabba sitting over on one side, generally being subdued and pretty quiet, and the crazy crowd from *Trader Joe's* on the other side, whooping it up and acting like hyenas on speed. In between there were tons of empty tables and chairs. I guessed Donnelly was too embarrassed to go over and sit with his rowdy colleagues. He was a loner type anyway.

After I finished up my set to riotous applause from the drunken rowdies, I sat in the back and watched in horror as my tipsy mates heckled all the comics who followed me.

"We want Lance!!!" one of the drunk girls kept screaming whenever one of of the other comics would start his or her routine. This, of course, would set off the whole table, like a bunch of barking beagles, all of them producing their own peculiar yelp, their own peculiar howl.

I kept trying to signal to Donnelly to go over and quiet the mob down, but I was having a hard time getting my buddy's attention. Donnelly was half in the bag himself.

Whenever one of the comedians would come off stage after his routine, he would give me a nasty look and say, "Nice friends, BB. Really nice friends." BB was my nickname. Everybody called me that.

It was, hands down, the worst night of my infant comedic career. I was trying to break into this business, make some meaningful contacts, show off my stuff, and my pals were killing me, making everyone else on the New York comedy circuit, at least those at the club that night, hate my guts.

I know that there's no controlling life, and that I've had more than my fair share of lumps, but I hope to hell that I never have to go through something like that again. It's was just horrific.

Chapter Thirteen

The old comedians, the ones who really know what they're doing, say never open with new material, always open with tried and true stuff, jokes that have worked for you in the past. Save the new stuff for the end of your routine. Get a few laughs with your sure-fire stuff and then try out the new material at the end.

You only have to make that mistake once or twice – kick off your gig with new jokes that you have never tried on anyone except your wife, your friends or your mirror – and you will learn very quickly to never, ever do that again.

The smell of death on stage is a frightening experience – it's called silence.

The one routine I always count on, always go to in a pinch, is my bit on the difference between men's rooms and women's rooms. Unless I've got a club full of young men, I routinely start with this bit before I try out any new material. Women seem to like it, especially since they can't figure out how I know that much about what goes on in their bathrooms. Thanks, Lettie.

Actually, I'm not at all sure that the bathroom bit is that funny (a lot of the laughs I get are for the jumping around and hamming it up that I do on stage during the routine). But it is original stuff, my very own creation, and it eventually became my trademark.

I became known on the New York comedy circuit as the guy who did the bathroom bit, as in: "We need another comic to fill out the lineup on Saturday night. You know of anybody good?"

"How about the guy who does the bathroom bit? What about him?"

That's how I got my nickname: BB. Not because when I was a

little boy I used to shoot the gun that all young boys shot back then. Not because I loved the great blues guitarist who could make his instrument weep and wail. And not because my favorite weekend pastime was holding up with Lettie in one of those quaint little inns that dot the New England countryside.

No, I became BB because I did toilet humor, because I did the "Bathroom Bit."

"Guys, you ever go by the ladies' room at a club? It sounds like the frigging Parakeet Pavilion at the Bronx Zoo in there. 'Oh that's a nice dress.' 'I just love your hair.' 'What's this new guy Jimmy like?' It goes on and on.

"Ladies, you know what's going on over in the men's room? You know what we're talking about in there?

"Nothing. There's NO talking in the men's room. It's a mausoleum. You can hear a pin drop.

"When you go into the men's room, you report to your battle station, you keep your head up, your eyes straight ahead. You never look to the side. You certainly never look to the side and down. And you never, ever look straight down. That would be the creepiest of all.

"And we have strict rules and regulations in the men's room. Man at urinal. Empty urinal. Man at urinal. Empty urinal. Man at urinal. Empty urinal. Right down the line. Every other one."

This is the part where I jump around, looking like I'm going from urinal to urinal.

"But there's always one jerk who screws it up, who leaves two urinals empty next to him.

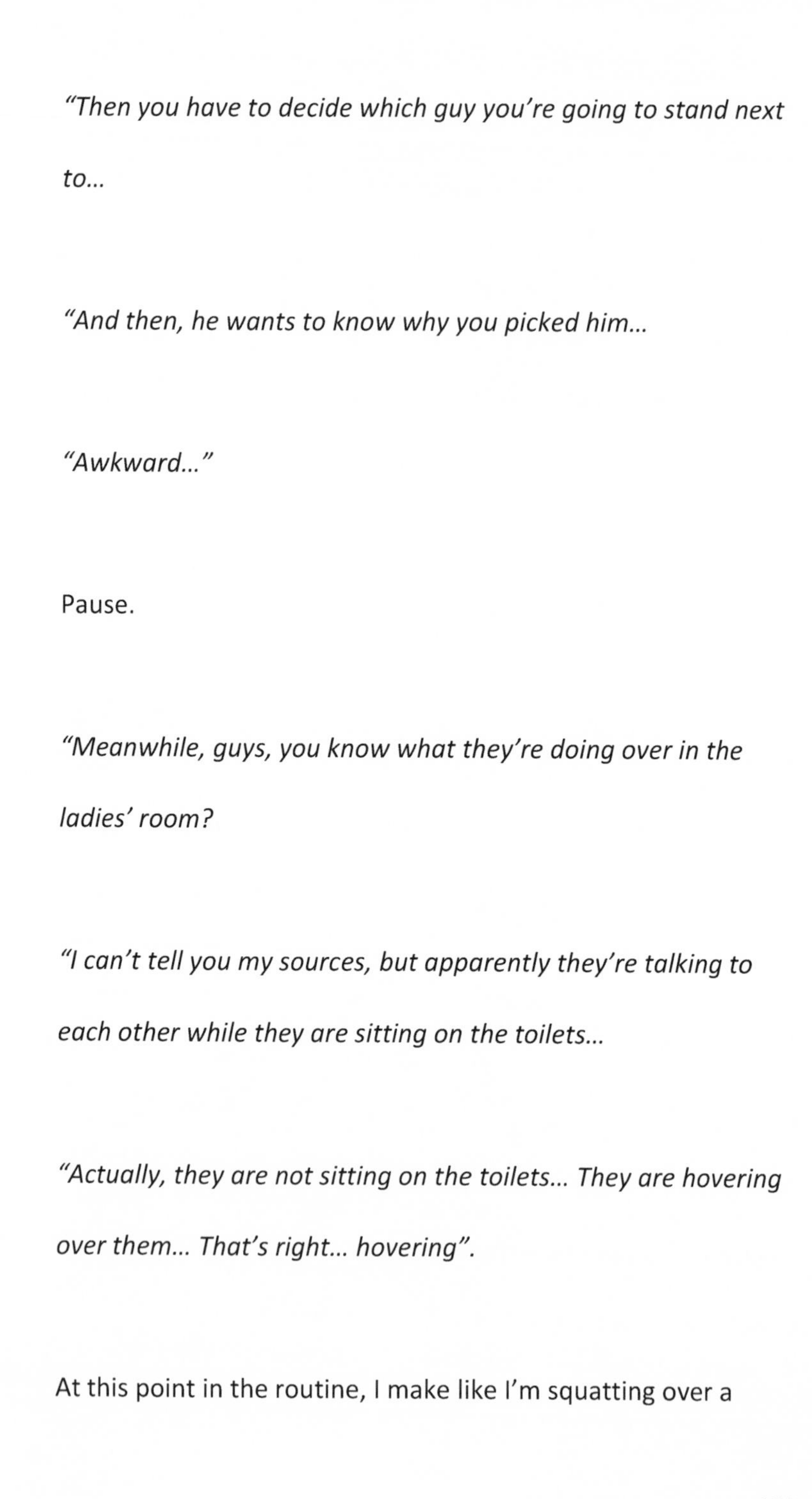

"Then you have to decide which guy you're going to stand next to...

"And then, he wants to know why you picked him...

"Awkward..."

Pause.

"Meanwhile, guys, you know what they're doing over in the ladies' room?

"I can't tell you my sources, but apparently they're talking to each other while they are sitting on the toilets...

"Actually, they are not sitting on the toilets... They are hovering over them... That's right... hovering".

At this point in the routine, I make like I'm squatting over a toilet.

"And then they do this strange thing where they make beehives by wrapping toilet paper around their hands... I'm not even sure what that's all about. It's some kind of alien thing they thought up...

"And then, one of them will say: 'Hey I think I might not have enough TP over here, could you pass me some... under the stall wall?' And they will. They'll actually pass the toilet paper right under the stall wall.

"Oh My God! Can you imagine if that ever happened in the men's room?

"Jesus, the next sound you would hear would be the sound of a steel boot crashing through your stall door and a fist slamming into the side of your head.

"'Did you just ask me for some TP?'

"'What the hell do I look like? A U.S. Senator?'"

"Listen, when we go in there, just remember no talking and no staring. Okay? We're clear, right?
Like Mommy says: 'Go in, do your business, get out. It's not supposed to be fun.'"

It was my first time ever, taking Dylan to the head, the first time Lettie trusted me enough to get the job done. Most of the time, I liked to do dad things. But for some reason, this chore – taking Dylan to the bathroom – had made me a nervous wreck.

But in we went, father and son on their maiden men's room voyage, a rite of passage for both. No sooner had we pulled up to the urinals, then Dylan stuck his head around one man's hip and blurted out: "Whoa. That's a big one. A lot bigger than yours, Dad!"

I grabbed Dylan by the hand and pulled him away quickly. "Remember no talking," I said to him, tossing a "sorry" over my shoulder to the man who was still doing his business.

"C'mon down here and pick out a spot," I said to Dylan as we marched down the row of urinals.

"No, don't stop at one of the ones that comes up to your chin," I pleaded. "And for God's sake, don't pick up those round, white things in there. No, those are not the world's largest breath mints! Go down to the end. That's right, the little guy urinal down there on the end."

I paused as Dylan stood in front of the urinal.

"Now pull down your zipper... No, NOT your pants for goodness sake... Just the zip... No, No, No, NOT YOUR UNDERWEAR TOO!!!"

But it was too late. Dylan was standing there, with his cute, nude little butt sticking out, his pants and underwear down around his ankles. I took my son by his shoulders. "Pull them back up," I said. "Pull your pants back up! And then pull your zipper down."

But by now, most of the men in the men's room were starting to wonder if it wasn't me who was a bit strange. Nobody talks in the men's room and here was this clown jabbering away. And what was he doing over there with the kid with no pants on?

"C'mon, kid," I pleaded. "Let's get this done, okay?"

Dylan had his pants up and zipper down, finally. Ready for action.

"Go ahead, point it in the urinal. No. No! NO! Don't turn towards me. Now, look what you've done. I'm sopping wet. Point it back in the urinal. NOW!"

Dylan was giggling. He thought it was funny that he had peed on his dad. But men don't like to hear giggling in the men's room. It pretty much creeps them out. We were getting a lot of stares.

"Dylan," I whispered loudly. "Hurry up and finish going... No, I know you have a lot. I can see that. And no, I don't care what you do as long as you stay in the urinal. Sure, make some designs, some figure eights. Whatever. Just hurry up and finish."

"You done?" I asked finally. "Now, shake it a couple of times and pull up your zipper. No, don't keep shaking it. Please, don't keep shaking it. Please stop playing with it!"

Dylan panicked at this point. He yanked up his zipper and did something that all guys do at least once in their lives. It's usually only once in their lives because it is the most painful thing any man can ever do to himself. Dylan caught his winkie in his zipper.

Out came a blood-curdling scream, followed by a tsunami of tears.

“Owwwwwwwwwwwwwwwwww!!!!!!!!!!!!!!!!!!!!!!!!!!!!!!!!”
Dylan wailed.

“It’s okay,” I said, sweeping him up in my arms. “It’s okay!!!”

But there was no consoling Dylan. He was a giant mess, a giant, hot, smoldering mess.

I put him back on the ground, quickly got his penis out of his zipper (it hadn’t gotten stuck too badly), pulled up his drawers, gathered him up, and raced out of the rest room, leaving a startled group of men behind.

But who should be waiting for us as we exited the rest room?

Mom.

"Oh My God!" Lettie was wailing now too. "What in the world have you done to our son?"

"Uhhhh... uhhhh..." I sputtered.

Lettie ripped Dylan out of my arms and took him into hers.

"Oh you poor, poor thing," she whispered into Dylan's tiny ears. "You poor, poor thing..."

She was cooing now, and Dylan was slowly but surely coming back down to earth. Lettie looked at me the whole time she was trying to comfort him. She was not happy. Finally, she spoke.

"What the hell happened in there?" she asked. "I have been

taking him into the ladies room for two years without incident. The first time you take him into the men's room, he comes out a cripple."

There was no comeback. No easy out. I threw myself on my sword.

"I screwed up." I said feebly. "I didn't mean to, but I screwed up."

Dylan and I were not allowed to go to the bathroom together again for six months.

Mad as Lettie was that day, I actually didn't think I was ever going to be trusted with Dylan again, at least not until he was shaving or something.

Chapter Fourteen

When Roscoe tells a joke, it is like getting hit in the head with a wet sack of ham hocks. Splat! Hot and heavy. You can't get out of the way of one of his jokes, even when you see it coming a mile away.

"What is it with sushi? Why are people always trying to get me to try it? They say: 'How do you know you won't like it until you try it?'

"Well, I haven't ever stuck ice picks in my eyes either. But I'm pretty sure, I wouldn't like it.

And I haven't ever buffed my balls with an electric sander, but I'm pretty sure I wouldn't like it.

And I've never been to a Jonas Brothers concert, but I'm pretty sure I wouldn't like it."

Roscoe rocks the house in my book. He is as old school as you can get. He appeals to an older audience, but he can win a few chuckles from the younger set as well. He wins them over, particularly women, because he is so earnest at what he does, so cute in a gruff, ol' bear kind of a way.

He looks like the famous country singer Kenny Rogers, maybe even a little bit like the Travelocity gnome as well, the one in the television commercials. But he attacks comedy, like a professional bowler. Set up the pins. Knock 'em down. Set up the pins. Knock 'em down.

In golf, they would have called him a "grinder," somebody who never quits, somebody who always gets the job done, somebody who just keeps plugging away, no matter what. You never had to worry about Roscoe. He may not bring the house down every time, but he always delivers, a good, competent set. And I would rather work with someone like that than have to rely on somebody who is hit or miss.

"You know if Kellogg's had any sense at all, they wouldn't have fired Olympic swimmer Michael Phelps for having a bong hit. I mean who do they think is eating Frosted Flakes anyway? Stoners.

"If Kellogg's had any sense at all, they would put a picture of Phelps and Tony the Tiger on the front of their cereal boxes smoking a joint together and saying: "This shit is Grrrrrrrrrrrrrreat!!!"

It might sound glamorous, playing in those New York night clubs, standing up there in front of the lights. But it's not. Not even close.

At night, the places can look pretty damn inviting, twinkly lights on the marquee outside, dark seductive cocktail tables and mood lighting on the inside. But these places are like the city of

New Orleans. She looks so good at night, with the bright lights on Bourbon Street, all that music drifting out into the street. Everybody looks like they are having such a good time. You even start to think: hey, maybe I could live here full-time.

Then, you get up the next morning and head out into her waiting arms, looking for more of that Southern loving, looking for more of that sweet romance you embraced the night before. But Bourbon Street in New Orleans is the pits in the morning. Piss and vomit stinking up the streets. No one is up, and they won't be up until well after noon, at the earliest. They're all hung over, trying to figure out who've they woken up next to and why.

No, Miss New Orleans is not so hot looking in the bright sunlight of day. She looks like a morning after hooker, her lipstick and eyeliner blotchy, smudged, and missing the mark, absurdly drawn all over her haggard face. Now we see what we didn't see the night before, the wrinkles, the worn lines, the pain she has endured over the years. Now we know why the Animals wrote that haunting song about her, about The *House of The Rising Sun*.

It's the same with the comedy clubs. At night-time, they are glittering palaces of laughter and good times, rooms where lovers wet their lips, where eyes shine with mirth in the dark, where clinking glasses and noisy communion combine to entertain and enthrall.

But during the day, they are just like New Orleans. They are -- all of them, even the high-end ones -- dives, black, dark, smelly rooms, cheap space, with plywood bathroom doors, and stinky toilets, death on parade, every expense spared, everything set up to maximize revenue, minimize costs, and deliver the profits.

Yep, you have to hand it to comedy clubs. Just like New Orleans, they sure do dress up good in the shadows of the night.

"Can you do a Friday nighter at 8 p.m.?" Roscoe wanted to know. "Broadway Comedy Club in midtown."

"Is it a bringer?" I asked. I didn't mind performing, particularly if I was going to get paid, but I didn't feel like bugging my friends to come see me again. It gets to be kind of embarrassing after a while, always asking your pals to come see you when they've been to see you a bunch of times already.

"Yeah, it's a bringer," he said. "But I can get you $25 for doing the show."

Twenty-five bucks. Be still my heart. I'll try not to spend it all at McDonalds before the subway ride home.

But it is always fun to work with Roscoe, and twenty-five bucks is twenty-five bucks. Forty bucks gross, really, if you think about it, since there is no way in hell I was ever going to pay taxes on my club earnings. Uncle Sam never seemed to me to have much of a sense of humor. So why should I give the government anything for exercising mine?

"Okay, I'm in," I said. "Who else is performing?"

"Daisy. Sly. I've got to find a couple more people," Roscoe said, and then sensing what I was about to ask, he added: "No, I'm really not interested in Margie performing. No offense. I just don't think he fits in with what I'm trying to do here."

"That's she."

"Huh?"

"She's a she. Margie's a she."

"Oh c'mon, man, if that's a she, then I'm a she."

"Suit yourself, doll face," I teased him. "See you Friday night."

Daisy is what guys used to call "dim" or "dizzy" when I was growing up, a cute girl with Heidi-like braids, giant blue eyes, and a dainty little ski-jump nose. She appears to be completely, or almost completely, clueless.

She actually wears lederhosen and Edelweiss blouses to perform in. I think she might actually believe that she is Heidi, and not just some girl from upstate New York who spent enough nights in the back of Flower Power mini-vans smoking herb to qualify as one of the original groupies for the Grateful Dead.

She is adorable, of course. Her timing is pretty bad, but getting better. Her material is whimsical and, usually, not terribly clever. But there is just something about her, her blinding innocence, her genuine naiveté, that makes audiences want to gobble her up, take her home with them.

"Oh don't be silly, you guys" she says in one of her routines. *"Cocaine isn't addictive. I've been using it every day for years."*

It is her little girl giggle that sells the joke. It is her little girl giggle that brings them back for more.

Sly is an angry black man. A really, really, funny, angry black man.

He actually plays off of this quite a bit. In fact, it's how he makes his living, playing off his righteous black anger.

"It's easier to be a black comedian than a white comedian," he confided to me one time outside the club. "You white folks are terrified of black people, and you'll laugh your asses off at anything we say, just as long as you think it will keep the black man from getting angry or upset. Nothing scares you more than an angry black man. You white people like your darkies to smile, look like they're happy, show off their pearly whites, just like OJ Simpson and Magic Johnson."

He had a point. You have a black man and a white man deliver the same joke, and the black man will get the bigger laugh every time, at least that's been my experience.

"And that's the way it should be, you motherfucking cracker," he said to me, making his eyes as big and white and scary as possible. "After everything you people have done to us, you owe us."

Then, he paused for dramatic effect and let the tension build.

“As far as I’m concerned, you honkies can pay me back in the comedy clubs. One fucking dollar at a time.”

How can you not dig Sly? He is the coolest guy I’ve ever met.

Chapter Fifteen

Sometimes, I miss her so much I don't feel like I can keep on breathing. The pain in my chest is so acute, I just want to give up, cave in, roll up in a ball in the corner and whimper away the rest of my life.

Dylan misses Lettie too, but in his own way.

"Mommy was born on October 14th, right?"

"Oh course, Dylan. Why are you asking? You already know the answer. When was the last time, you got a date wrong?" I looked up over my reading glasses at my son. "Unless you're just trying to play a joke on me."

Dylan liked to do that to me, every once in a while, intentionally mess up a date, just to see if I was paying attention; intentionally make a mistake like saying "murter," instead of "murder" just to get a big laugh.

"She would be 32 and seven months old today," he said, without emotion.

"That's right," I replied.

"Grandma and Grandpa must have made her in the spring, in February," Dylan said.

"That's right, Dylan."

"You and Mommy made me in August, right Dad?" Dylan continued, matter-of-factly.

I wondered why my son didn't show any of the same angst, the same emotional upheaval, that I did when talking about Lettie? She wasn't just a bunch of numbers, kid, not just a bunch of statistics. She was your mother. She was my wife.

Dylan could see my face. It was not the way it usually was. He paused a minute and looked at me intently.

"She should be with us, right? She should still be with us, shouldn't she?" Dylan said.

I was crushed.

"Yes, son, she should."

Golf -- humorist and author Mark Twain once lamented -- is a perfectly good walk spoiled.

But one day, it hit me. Fuck the walk. Let my 11-year-old son drive a cart.

It was brilliant. Dylan would never be able to drive a car, but he'd get the same pleasure and experience, bopping around in a golf buggy. And it worked.

Dylan loved driving the cart, trying to keep it on the skinny asphalt paths. It took him a while, but Dylan got pretty good at it. The golf cart was perfect for him. He couldn't get into too much trouble with a cart because it couldn't go too fast. It has a governor that controls the speed.

If there was something tricky, like a hill, then he would pretend to panic a little. Actually, he'd start shrieking with laughter, all part of his macabre "we're going to die, we're going to die" sense of humor.

But while he was shrieking, Dylan would stop steering the golf cart, take one foot off the gas, and the other foot off the brake. I would feign hysteria from my side of the cart. "What are you doing?" I would yell.

But we both knew that we didn't have anything to worry about. The great thing about a golf cart is that it has automatic brakes. If you take your foot off the accelerator, it stops itself. Just kind of poops out and stops.

There aren't a whole lot of golf courses where Dylan and I live in Astoria, in fact there aren't any, so we have to take the subway out to the public golf course in Brooklyn.

Roscoe and Sly come out and meet us sometimes. None of us are any good at golf, myself included, but it is a fun way to hang out, guy style. We tell jokes in between shots, work on our material, and bitch and moan about women. Well, at least, Sly and Roscoe do. I've been more circumspect since Lettie died.

"BB," Sly winked at me. "I hope Dylan isn't planning on crashing one of those buggies, cause we ain't got no insurance."

"I won't crash it," Dylan said confidently. "I can drive very well."

Dylan was in Seventh Heaven. He just loved hanging out with the guys, gobbling up every word, every joke that was uttered. And the amazing thing was, the kid never forgot any of them.

I can remember every shot, on every hole. But I'll be damned if I can remember three of the twenty-five jokes that are told while we are out on the course on any given day.

Dylan on the other hand can do both, recall every one of my shots and every one of the jokes, word for word.

"What should I hit here, Dylan?" I would ask Dylan, the human memory machine.

"You normally hit a 5-wood, Dad," Dylan would say solemnly.

"Then you definitely don't want to hit that club," Roscoe would quip. "Not if that's the one you usually use. Cause that club is not your friend."

"Never mind about that," Sly would jump in. "Let him hit what he wants. Cause that club is definitely <u>our</u> friend."

Sly and Roscoe will do anything to win a bet, including psychological warfare; never mind that the winner can pocket no more than six dollars for the day, even if everything goes his way.

If Dylan weren't here, I thought, I would lay these guys out with some choice words, but I decided instead to take the ribbing straight up, without cursing in front of my son.

"Dylan, could you please hand your father his trusty 5-wood so that he can show these fools the proper use of said club?" I lampooned, hoping against hope that I would "pure" a shot with the club that the famous golfer Gene Sarazen used when he hit a shot at The Masters that was so good it was appropriately labeled "the shot heard round the world."

But, ladies and gentlemen, I am no Gene Sarazen. I over-swung and dribbled the ball 75 yards down the fairway into a sand trap. With Dylan there, I couldn't even say "shit." I had to hold it in and jump back in the cart, sulking.

Sly could see I was dying to let out a stream of high-pitched expletives after my pathetic shot. *"Why do they call it golf?"* he smiled without sympathy. *"All the other four letter words were taken."*

But Dylan has always been oblivious to, or at least unconcerned about, my shortcomings as a golfer.

"Jump in, BB," he says, revving up the cart and laughing because he knows he can sneak in my nickname while the guys are around and I won't be able to stop him.

The public course where we play is almost as big a dive as the clubs we perform in. There are hard, bare, brown clay spots all over the place, broken glass and nails everywhere, rocks and pebbles coming out the wazoo, and sand traps that are more likes quarries than bunkers.

Surly golf rangers come around, barking at golfers to "hurry up, hurry up." The ranger is just doing his job, but there is no reason to hurry up because on this municipal golf track, there is no place to go. It always seems like half the men of Brooklyn and Queens are out there playing on any given day. A round can take up to five and a half, even six, hours.

Actually, I don't mind the delays too much. It gives all of us a chance to shoot the shit, goof around and tell jokes.

Roscoe can be especially funny on the golf course, not necessarily when he is telling jokes, or working on his routine, but just when he's going off about his life, usually about his marriage to Sheryl. They have been married 27 years, fighting constantly, but everyone knows they wouldn't have a clue what to do without each other.

The other day, Roscoe started to launch into one of my favorite, all-time jokes, but one I didn't think would be particularly appropriate for Dylan to hear. But there is no stopping Roscoe once his joke train has left the station.

So one guy says to other: "I had a terrible Freudian slip the other day. I was at the airline ticket counter, and there was this incredibly lush babe behind the counter with an enormous rack. I got so flustered, I asked her for 'Two pickets to Tits-burgh."

"Oh, I know just what you mean," said the other guy. "I had a Freudian slip of my own the other day at breakfast. I meant to

say to my wife: 'Please pass me the sugar,' but it came out: 'You fucking cunt, you ruined my life!'"

Actually, Roscoe didn't use the C-word in front of Dylan, he substituted the B-word instead. Not great, but much better.

I hate the C-word. It is so evil. At the same time, I have to admit that that word makes that particular joke. Sometimes a joke just takes precedent over civility, at least for comedians it does. Maybe that's why we're always in trouble, or about to be in trouble. Maybe that's why people laugh, because they see us playing so close to the edge.

What came out next made all of us double over.

"That's a good joke, Roscoe" Dylan said, with a totally straight face. "But that's the first time I've ever heard it without the word 'cunt' in it."

Chapter Sixteen

Slosser is my secret weapon.

He is the camera guy, the guy who takes videos of comics' performances at various clubs around town. He charges $10 per comic per gig. Slosser is not going to get rich anytime soon, but he is a good guy, another hanger-on in the rodeo of fools that comprise the comedy circuit.

Slosser is a marginally shy, quintessentially short, nerd. There is no other way to put it. He wears the same blue jeans, holes and all, every night, along with one of his rock 'n roll tee-shirts featuring one of his favorite bands. He has big, black rim glasses that seem to swallow up most of his face. He is the kind of guy you would pass on a street in New York and never even notice.

But I know that as a comic the way to get better is by watching Slosser's videos. They aren't very well shot, kind of grainy with bad sound, but they do give me the ability to watch my show later on and make necessary adjustments to my act.

I don't know how the older generation of comics did it. I don't know how they could get any better if they never got a chance to see themselves perform.

I also like having Slosser watch my routines while he is filming them. Slosser has a nearly identical sense of humor as mine, and he actually laughs aloud when he thinks one of my jokes is funny. A cameraman is not supposed to do that. He's supposed to control himself, keep from breaking up when the entertainer's up there doing his thing. It can ruin the soundtrack that accompanies the video when he laughs.

A lot of guys don't want to work with Slosser, don't like the idea of paying someone to shoot their performances. They'd rather figure it out themselves. But Slosser is okay in my book. I figure I probably owe as much of my career to Slosser as to anyone else, him and that cheap ass video camera of his.

Slosser goes to all of *Rush's* concerts when they come to in New York every year. I mean every concert, all four of them, every year, without fail. I usually let him drag me along to one of them.

"Do you believe this?" Slosser gets so excited when the Canadian rock group comes to town. "Do you fucking believe this?"

I think it is kind of fun to see him get all excited like that, all pumped up to see the same show that we've seen a billion times before. Actually, the shows aren't exactly the same. The music, and Slosser's reaction to it, is generally the same. But the shows are actually a little bit different year to year.

I have to hand it to *Rush*. They do know how to entertain. They use all kinds of cool pyro and video and animation, and they always play for about three hours. That's a long time for a rock concert.

I can't imagine how hard it would be to entertain for that long. I can barely hold up my end for 10-15 minutes.

Slosser is so nuts about *Rush* that he even made me go see a bromance movie about two guys who shared a love for *Rush* so strong it included both of them memorizing all of the group's lyrics. *Rush* has put out a ton of albums over the years, so we're talking about a lot of lyrics.

It's safe to say that Slosser knows all their lyrics too, which is kind of weird because he wasn't even born when they first started playing back in the 70s.

A *Rush* concert is always a tribute to maleness. Thousands and thousands of black tee-shirts, a sea of them. Pretty much all guys. There was actually a pretty funny scene in a video at this year's *Rush* concert where the band members were talking back stage about how many girls showed up at their concert.

"There must have been seven of them tonight, all in the front row," one member said.

"Yeah," another said. "A record!"

Mona was busting some kid's chops pretty badly.

"Look, I don't make the rules," she said. "You told me that you thought you could bring 10 people to tonight's show. You brought none. Last week, you also told me you could bring 10 people. You brought two. I'm not running a charity here"

She paused and put her hands on her broad hips. “You hear what I’m saying.”

Poor bastard.

This is not a pleasant business, this comedy business, not a pleasant business at all.

“I’ll let you slide this one time,” Mona was saying to the new comic. “But you have got to start producing people. Do you hear me? Do we have an understanding?”

The young comic, a flashy gay guy who was really funny, really witty, was crestfallen. I sidled over to offer him some comfort, not something comics usually do for one another. Most of them shy away from the lame or wounded, don’t want to catch whatever they have, catch whatever it is that’s holding them back. Comedians are a very suspicious lot.

"Kid, hang in there," I said. "You're funny, really funny. You'll get your break."

The gay comic smiled a weak little smile, then nodded and said. "Thanks, BB. Appreciate it." But he didn't sound convinced.

I didn't blame Mona. After all, she has given me and the rest of the troupe a shot at the title, and she is entitled to make a living herself, just like everyone else. She is not making a lot of money doing this. She is doing this because she has the comedy bug herself and she can't get rid of it. She is doing this because she actually likes hanging around with all of us losers with dreams of making it big. That, and she likes to do stand-up herself. She likes to slot herself into a show, at least once a week, sometimes more.

Mona does not have an easy life herself. Try being a comic and a booker and an agent all at the same time. These clubs are the pits and the owners of them are even worse. But Mona knows what needs to be done to run a room on a shoestring. She's been around a long time. The old gal has some tricks up her sleeve, ways to boost the take, ways to cut down on costs.

For example, instead of taking her dresses to the dry cleaners where they charge her eight bucks apiece, she takes her clothes down to the Salvation Army where she'd drops them off once a week. She comes back a couple of days later, and, nine times out of ten, they are still there. But by now they are pressed and cleaned. She buys them back for four dollars apiece, saving four bucks a garment.

None of us ever stops to ponder or appreciate Mona's lot in life. At one time or another, each of us has bitched about how she makes all the money and doesn't pay any of us enough. Truth is, she's scraping by too.

I try to remember this sometimes. Life can look pretty damn different, depending on which angle you're coming from.

It's funny to watch comics get ready for a show. They all have their own styles, but they all do pretty much the same thing. They start to isolate and begin working on their lines over and over, trying to zone in on their routine, trying to practice their timing and get it down before the performance.

A lot of them will leave the club and wander around outside, lip synching their entire routine as they walk. They actually look like street people, schizophrenics, crazy folks, talking to themselves as they ramble along, waving their arms and gesturing, silently spouting their punch lines to no one in particular.

If you get two or three of them walking around the same block at the same time, you'd think there was a homeless convention in town or something.

Sometimes, these sidewalk warm-ups are even funnier than the shows themselves, especially if you've already heard every one's routine a million times before. Seeing them doing it as lip-moving street mimes before the show is priceless.

And if the pre-game festivities are funny, you haven't seen anything until you've sat through the post-game analysis. Ask any wife or girlfriend who has had to live for any length of time with a comic.

"How do you think I did tonight?" the comic will ask his significant other after the show.

"You did great, sweetie," she will say, having answered this question so many times, after so many gigs, that she could do it in her sleep.

"How was my timing?"

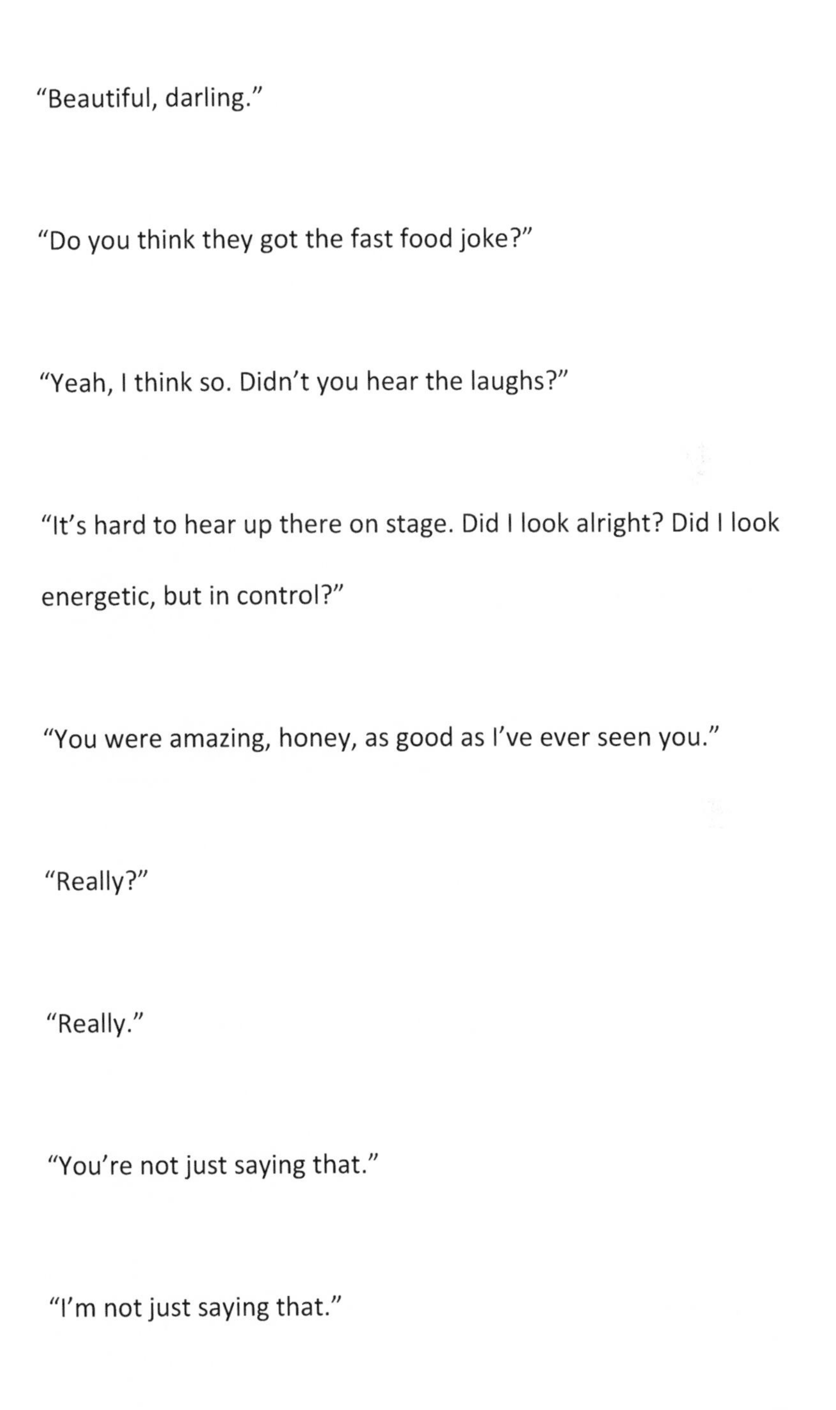

"Beautiful, darling."

"Do you think they got the fast food joke?"

"Yeah, I think so. Didn't you hear the laughs?"

"It's hard to hear up there on stage. Did I look alright? Did I look energetic, but in control?"

"You were amazing, honey, as good as I've ever seen you."

"Really?"

"Really."

"You're not just saying that."

"I'm not just saying that."

This can go on for hours. Comics are seriously twisted, insecure people. They need constant attention and affection. Otherwise, they wither up and die.

And the truth is, they don't always give back as much as they receive. In fact, to be honest, they never give back as much as they receive. They can't. They are just too self-centered and too self-absorbed. That's just the way it is.

So be forewarned if you want to fall in love with a comedian, it's not going to be a picnic.

Chapter Seventeen

Margie said Dylan was playing with himself pretty much around the clock. I wasn't sure how she knew that, but I didn't want to get into it with her, right this second.

"Do you want me to speak to him?" she asked me.

Oh yeah, Margie, I thought, I want the transgender nanny who looks like a pro wrestler to give my 13-year-old autistic son sex education lessons. Oh Lettie, where are you when I need you?

But I didn't have any better answers to hand.

"Maybe you want Roscoe to talk to him," she said, sensing my hesitation. I knew she was starting to work up a major league resentment. "Maybe you want that Neanderthal to screw up young Dylan but good with his grotesque interpretation of what men and women should do to each other."

I was never any good at standing up to women, especially if they had been men before.

"Well, what would you tell Dylan? How would you explain things to him?" I asked, stalling for time.

"I would tell him that God gave him his sexuality and wants him to have fun with it," Margie said, triumphantly. "I would tell him that we live in a strange world, where people can't deal with their feelings and so they try to conceal them by judging others."

She was on a roll.

"For that reason, Dylan, you have to be extra careful to keep things like masturbation and playing with yourself -- which are perfectly natural and God-given -- to yourself so that you don't give people out there ammunition to make fun of you," she concluded.

Wow. Dylan would understand that explanation in a heartbeat. People had been making fun of him his whole life. Margie had a way about her, a wisdom that wasn't apparent from an initial meeting.

"Thanks, Margie," I said. "I would be most grateful if you could have a chat with Dylan."

And that's how my son got his first lesson on the birds and the bees. From Margie, a transgender comedian.

Margie had been a real sweetheart while Dylan and I had been going through the early days of our post-Lettie life.

"Nothing's going to happen to you," she would say to me when she could tell I was worried about Dylan's future. "You're a young man. You've got a long time to live. Besides, if anything does happen to you, I can always look after Dylan."

That was nice of her to say. She is a real pal, that Margie.

And who's to say, if I did die, maybe Margie and Dylan would be perfect together, maybe my son would be even better off with her.

Chapter Eighteen

It was my birthday so the guys that I worked with down at *Trader Joe's*, and the gang of comics I hung out with, decided to throw me a surprise party downstairs in a little bar at Comix, a comedy club not too far from the meat-packing district.

It was late in the evening, but they brought Dylan along with them anyway. He was at the age where socializing was getting a little more tolerable, maybe even a little bit interesting, and he could handle group sings, even "Happy Birthday," without losing his grip.

"So how does it feel to be 36?" Daisy asked me in her adorable, little girl's voice.

"Just peachy," I replied.

"He won't be celebrating a birthday again on a Tuesday until 2019," Dylan said matter-of-factly to no one in particular.

"He'll probably still be working in the produce section at *Trader Joe's* and holding up the number eight slot at Gotham's in 2019," quipped Sly. "Sorry ass, no talent, honky loser bastard."

"Glad you could make it," I winked at Sly.

"No worries, man," said Sly. "Us black people don't start our chicken and watermelon eating, and listening to all that soul-destroying rap music, until much later in the evening, so I was free to come by for a little while."

It was a special night. Even Roscoe and Margie were being civil to one another. I thought it might have been because they were both bitching about where Mona had put them in last Saturday night's line-up.

"That woman is clueless," Roscoe was waxing. "She has no idea how to fill out a good line-up."

"She is limited," Margie agreed, completely unaware that she and Roscoe were both thinking the same thing at the same time. Each of them was sure that he or she should have been the evening's headliner.

Donnelly could get fed up with comics pretty easily. He found them tedious and frankly, not all that funny. But even he was on his best behavior that night. He knew it was my birthday and this group meant a lot to me, so he was laying off his usual sarcastic comments. He wasn't even bitching about Slosser filming the whole thing.

Despite all the laughter and the fun jokes and the ribbing and having Dylan there way past his bedtime, I felt lonely, really, really lonely.

I hate times like these, when I'm at the center of everyone's attention, and then, all of a sudden, for no apparent reason, all the yelling and screaming and back-slapping seems to fade into the background, like my ears have been muffled or something and the lights have dimmed. The whole world seems to dissolve and disappear around me. I just feel like crying, just feel like breaking down and packing it all in.

I knew why. I missed Lettie, missed her with an anguish too intense to extinguish.

"Dad, are you alright?" It was Dylan.

"Yeah, son, I'm good." I said. "Thanks for asking."

But Dylan could see the truth, the real truth. He could see the woman in the gorilla suit. He could see what was really going on.

"You miss Mommy?" he asked, without expression.

I almost broke down. I could barely speak.

"Yeah, I do, kid, I really do," I whispered.

"Me too, Dad," Dylan said in his mechanical way. "I miss her just as much as you do."

We sat and stared at each other for a few minutes.

Finally, Dylan said: “I think you’ve had enough birthday for one night.”

Then, with a huge shit-eating grin, he added, staring right into my eyes: “We’ve got to get out of this place. It’s murter in here!”

We both collapsed into laughter, hugging each other, and rocking back and forth, reduced to tears of belly-aching hilarity.

Lettie doesn’t have birthdays anymore.

It’s a crying shame. No one appreciated birthdays more than Lettie. She reveled in them, loved the celebration of life, the progression of years, the human growth that accompanies the anniversary of one's passing into the next phase of existence.

"This is the only October 14th, 2006, there will ever be," she enthused when she woke up on her last birthday. "We should make the most of it."

Lettie awakened every morning in a terrific mood, leaping out of bed, throwing open the windows, talking a mile a minute about her plans for the day. My inclination in the morning is to pull the covers up under my chin, roll over and try to blot the world out for as long as possible. I dread the moment when I am finally forced to let go of my pillows and arise.

Her last birthday before her death was a study in her annual embrace of her special day. She insisted that the three of us rent a car, and drive out to the country to pick apples and go for a hike amongst the colored leaves of mid-autumn.

"Isn't this divine?" she asked, her mouth making a funny, little twist, a cute little twist that became her hallmark tic while growing up. “Don’t you wish this day would last forever?”

Dylan was all in, even if he didn’t show it, didn’t smile much. The bright foliage that hadn’t drifted to earth, and the dead leaves that had, intrigued him. He shuffled his feet along, consumed with the rustling, crackly sound he made while walking through the woods.

Protected against the cool mountain breeze by her L.L. Bean flannel shirt and tight fitting Wrangler blue jeans, Lettie joined her son, grabbing his hand with one of her own, and tousling his hair with the other. “Isn’t this amazing? How lucky are we? We have the whole trail to ourselves.”

Such joy, such unbridled gratitude and passion! How could you not love her?

And then, it happened.

Not twenty-five yards in front of us, a massive, furry black figure emerged from a battery of bushes. It stumbled onto the path, turned, stopped and stared right at us. It was a giant black bear. I am talking, a huge, black bear. I bet if he had stood up he'd have been a foot taller than me, and I'm 6 foot-one.

We froze in our tracks.

As a confirmed city slicker I was not sure what to do, but I had read somewhere that the last thing you want to do with a bear is turn and run. Hold your ground, I vaguely remember the literature saying, and make some noise. But I didn't. I couldn't. Neither could Lettie and Dylan.

We just stood there silently and stared right back at the bear. He continued to stare at us.

Nothing happened for the next few minutes. It seemed like an eternity. I kept praying the whole time that Dylan wouldn't do something to anger the beast, but I didn't have to. Dylan was completely engrossed in the moment, completely and utterly intrigued by the unexpected event. He was clearly not afraid.

And oddly enough, neither was Lettie. She had an enormous grin on her face. It appeared only I was scared shitless by the menacing creature.

After a time, probably a minute or so, the bear, who had seated himself in the middle of the trail shortly after the stand-off began, raised up, gave us one last look, and a snort, and then lumbered off into the woods, covered quickly by the shoulder-high shrubbery that adorned the trail. He didn't seem to be very impressed with us. I guess he thought: the naked ones just aren't that interesting.

"Was that amazing or what?" Lettie said, overcome by emotion. "He was so majestic, so regal. And did you see that coat, so shiny, black and beautiful. I can't believe it. What a treat!"

"He was very large," Dylan said. "Very large for a black bear, mother. Most of the black bears in this part of New Jersey are much smaller. At least that's what I learned in a book." I guess I wasn't the only who had been reading about bears.

"Thank you, God! Thank you, God!" Lettie rejoiced. "What a special day! Best birthday ever!"

Today was not a special day for me. Today would have been her 38th birthday.

Chapter Nineteen

Abruptly, one day, Mona announced she was giving Dylan a job, just a little something on the side to keep him busy. He could sweep and clean up before and after the performances.

"I can't pay him anything, of course," she said, in her usual way. "I'd love to, but you know how strict those child labor laws are." She had a point. He was only 14.

Pay aside, I was immensely grateful that she was letting Dylan learn a skill, any skill at all, a skill that might someday unlock the door of employment for him.

"He's going to have to be here early, around 8 p.m. on weekend nights, and he won't get off until after 10 p.m.," she said. "You cool with that?"

"Yeah, I'm cool with that," I said.

I knew this was maybe not my best plan ever, having my kid hanging around a night club, with all the drinking and stuff that goes on. But, I consoled myself, at least the mayor banned smoking a few years back.

Lettie would never have gone for this, letting a young teenager, barely out of puberty, stay out on a school night in a comedy club, listening to a bunch of clown boys, and girls, spitting out lame jokes, most of them dripping with sexual innuendo, and more than occasionally, curse words.

But I actually liked having him nearby. He was the only thing I had left in life and I couldn't ever spend enough time with him. And I was hoping that if Dylan got good enough at cleaning up around the club, maybe we could try to get him a similar job down at *Trader Joe's* later on. That way I could keep an eye on him, work with him and see him all the time.

I was obsessed with trying to find a skill for Dylan, something that he could translate into income, something that would protect him if God and the Fates suddenly decided to take away his other parent.

Besides, with Margie and me both working the Friday and Saturday rooms on Mona's roster, there was no one to take care of Dylan at home. I sure as hell couldn't afford a sitter. Having Dylan around would take care of that problem.

I knew I owed Mona big time.

Chapter Twenty

It came out of nowhere and, while a big shot in the arm both ego-wise and financially, it was going to be tricky.

The Big Apple Comedy Club asked me if i wanted to run their room on Thursday nights. With this job, I would finally be able to quit at *Trader Joe's* and focus on comedy full-time. I'd have to manage and recruit comedians, which was always a trial of patience and nerves. But because I would be the boss, I would be able to guarantee myself a slot in the line-up for every Thursday night. With some luck, I might even make enough money to start saving up for a vacation with Dylan, maybe even buy a car.

But if I took the job, there were a couple of things to worry about: Mona first, and then my fellow comics, especially Margie.

Mona ran Saturday nights at the same club, as well as Friday nights at another club. As cool as it would be to a booker, pulling in the talent and controlling the line-up, I would have to think this one through. If I took this job and fell flat on my face, Mona would never, ever give me another shot, never, ever let me come back and play one of her shows again.

Another thing. If I took the job, I would be the competition to some degree. Mona and I wouldn't be competing on the same nights, but we would be drawing from the same talent pool of performers.

There were more than enough comics out there to go around. But most of them were not quality performers. And I didn't want to put on some half-assed show. If I took this job, I wanted to run the best room in the city.

And therein lay the rub.

What was I supposed to tell Margie when she asked me if she

could be in my line-up? "You're not good enough for me. Never mind that you look after my kid every day, I don't think you can cut it".

And how about Roscoe? He was a class performer, and solid as the day is long. But he'd been around a few years now. How many bums was he going to put in seats? How many new faces was he going to bring to the table? I was starting to feel like management scum, one of those guys who is only concerned about himself. But I knew that getting fannies in seats was the way I would make money, by having my comics bring in people who could pay cover charges and buy drinks.

But I was not at all sure I wanted to deal with those issues. I was not sure I wanted to tackle my friends head on, or listen to them bitch about how I would be taking home all the money while they starved, and how I didn't have a clue as to how to make out a line-up card that was worth a damn.

Another thing to consider was Dylan. I couldn't believe I had forgotten about him. If I took the Thursday night gig, Mona would be sure to fire Dylan as her clean-up guy, which would be a shame since he was really digging the job. That could be a major setback for Dylan's psyche, and a major setback for my plan to find him a longer-term occupational skill set. Dylan would need some sort of track record before he could get another job, and getting fired wasn't going to help.

Why did life have to be so complicated? Why did life have to be so hard? I was not sure I could take all this agro even if I was going to be making more bread.

And then, it came to me. Instead of guessing, why didn't I just take the issue to my pals and see what they had to say?

Dylan wanted me to take the job. Margie wanted me to take the job. Roscoe, Slosser and Daisy all wanted me to take the job.

Sly made a pretense out of saying: "Why should I support another white man's ascent to greatness?" But I knew deep down Sly wanted me to take the job too.

I just wondered if I could do it without ending up in a big pissing match with Mona, end up in a war I couldn't win.

"Why don't you just go to Mona and talk it over with her?" said Margie. "Maybe you two could work out a deal or something."

Oh yeah, Margie, great advice. Maybe I should just walk right into the lion's den, stick my frigging head in her mouth, and ask her to chomp down on it.

"If I did that, she'd think I already set this whole thing up beforehand, that I went behind her back, and that I'm being totally disloyal," I said.

"Well, you never know," Margie countered. "She might surprise you."

God, she sounded just like a wife, trying to be all encouraging and stuff, trying to find a way through the maze, acting like this was our collective problem, not just mine.

"I don't know," I said. "It's such a long shot. She could go ballistic."

"Well, you don't have a lot of choices, do you?" Margie said. "Maybe you should give it a try."

She gave me that heartfelt look that women give when they want you to give in, quit torturing yourself and try something new.

"I don't know," I said. "We'll see."

"What are you saying?"

"I'm saying we should think about partnering."

"Why? Why would I want to partner with you?" Mona looked pissed.

"Because you can't do it all by yourself. If you want to grow your business, you're going to need help," I said.

I knew Mona would be skeptical. She already had a business. Why would she want to share it with me?

"Besides," I jumped in again. "If we compete against each other, especially for talent, we might just end up screwing each other over. If we find a way to work together, maybe we can both survive and flourish." This last bit was 100 percent Margie's idea, the iron fist in the velvet glove approach, she called it.

Mona stared at me for a few minutes.

"How do you think it might work?" she said, finally.

I was in, in with a chance.

After endless discussions, Mona and I eventually settled on a plan. We would form a company, a company called Laugh Incorporated, not all that creative a name for a couple of people who were supposed to be creative, but it did accurately spell out who we were and what we wanted to do.

Mona would retain 67 percent ownership for her two nights. I would get 33 percent of our infant company for bringing in my one night. This was a generous offer on her part, given she had an established business and she had a Friday night show and a Saturday night show. I only had a Thursday night show. Thursday was a much harder night to pull people in compared to the weekends.

But here was the catch and why she did the deal.

Mona made me the new talent guy. That meant I would have to go out and find new comics to play all three of our shows. I would be doing all the heavy lifting. That's why she was willing to pay me a third. She was cutting her current workload big time and raking in dough on another night. It might even free her up to do some more comedy of her own, which could add to her weekly income.

During the negotiations, I found out a couple of things. First off, it turned out that contrary to what Mona had told me years ago when she first discovered me, she didn't actually have a legion of college kids running around the Internet looking for new talent. It was just her. She had been posturing, had been doing all the work herself. And now it was going to be part of my new job, a tedious, time-consuming part of my new job.

Secondly, because of this, I would have to go other comedy shows to scout talent. It wasn't that I minded going out and seeing shows. I can listen to comics twenty-four seven, three-six-five. The problem was Dylan. I didn't want to spend any more time away from him than necessary, plus I didn't want to burden Margie any more than she already was.

But it didn't matter what my concerns were. They – Margie and Dylan -- would have none of it, neither of them.

"Oh, BB," Margie said. "You have to go for it. This is your dream. You can't stay at that grocery store forever. You have to make this work." I could have sworn that I was talking to Lettie.

Dylan took me by surprise too. He sided with Margie. "Just do it, Dad," he said, with his usual direct, no nonsense monotone.

Chapter Twenty-One

I stood there, arms folded, looking at the piece of paper in his hand. My first line-up card. Can you believe it? How cool is this?

I had picked out a pretty good master of ceremonies, I thought. Myself.

That way I didn't have to pay anyone else to do the job and I could have a chance to try out a few jokes of my own in an opening monologue and in between my introductions of all the various performers.

Mona was not convinced that this was the best idea I had ever had, but she was going to let me have my way tonight because I had filled the room up, and filled it up with a crowd that was packing away the liquor pretty good, something that would please the club owner no end.

"We have a great show for you tonight," I heard myself saying. It was really bizarre to be in this position, trying to be the warm-up guy, the guy who got the crowd going from a cold start.

"So did you hear that Rio de Janeiro beat out Chicago for the Summer Olympics games?" I was out of the gate.

"Boy that was a tough call. Do you want to have the summer games in a place that parties all night, every night; a place where they make a sugar cane drink that will knock your block off, a place where every other person is wearing a thong bikini? Or do you want to have the games in a place where you can get a bratwurst and meet Mike Ditka?"

Nothing. Not even a snicker.

Great start to your new career, I thought. Way to go, Clown Boy.

It was times like these when a comic has to bear down, lean into the centrifugal force, turn in the direction of the skid. Every cell in your body is telling you to run for the door, to give up and pack it in. But you have to keep going. You have to keep the routine on track. Keep your timing. Don't speed up. Don't slow down. Don't overcompensate. Just keep working the gig the way you practiced it, the way you practiced it out there on the street before the show.

Somehow, I'm not sure how, I got through the opening monologue.

Thank God, I had Roscoe as the kickoff act. Roscoe didn't want to be the opener. No one does. It's just too early in the show. The crowd hasn't had a chance to relax yet, knock back a drink or two, and get into the rhythm of the evening.

But Roscoe did it for me, his buddy, and he did his usual solid job, bailing me out after my horrible opening MC segment. I was more comfortable after Roscoe's routine after he saved my ass.

I only told one joke as MC this time before quickly moving the show along by introducing the second comic with little fanfare.

He was a new kid, and of course, he had brought a bunch of his friends to see him, six or seven of them. Not nearly enough friends to win him a better slot than number two, but a respectable opening crowd nonetheless.

His pals whooped it up to beat the band. But the kid, a skinny little guy with a super thin tie and a ratty ski cap, was a nervous wreck, this being his first time on the big stage and all. At one point, I thought he was going to puke.

But in the end, I thought he did alright. The kid could keep coming back as far as I was concerned. He would improve. It would be interesting later on to see what Mona thought of him. She was standing over on the other side of the room near the curtain that hid Slosser and his video camera from the audience.

The number three and four slots are a comedian's ideal positions. The clientele has had time to settle in and have a few pops. They are not too drunk yet and they haven't started suffering from comedy fatigue, which comes from watching too many comics in a row.

I had taken something of a chance. I gave it to Daisy. Actually, it was not that big a chance. She may not have been my best act, but the room was filled with men, most of them aged 20-30, guys who had come to see their friends perform.

I had actually waited until the last second to decide who went into the coveted number three slot, but when I saw all those testosterone-producing machines out there in the darkness, I knew Daisy was the solution. She was so damn cute, I figured the men would gobble her up and beg for more. They did.

And Daisy was so grateful to be in a starring role that she put on one of the best shows I'd ever seen out of her. The crowd was roaring. It didn't matter that her jokes weren't that funny. She was their Heidi and they loved her.

Maybe the research was right. Maybe there is no connection between humor and laughter. Maybe all the guys were laughing, just because they were dying to get into Daisy's drawers.

In any event, she was over the moon when she came off stage. She couldn't have been happier. She flew off the wooden platform and planted a big, wet one on my lips. "Yippee," she squealed.

The number four slot was my headliner slot, the perfect place for Sly, who had been on fire recently. He'd even won a couple of low level television gigs on *Comedy Central* and *VH1*. Sly was outrageously hot again tonight, knocking it out of the park, an angry black man railing against the white universe. Chris Rock and Richard Pryor would have been proud.

I saved a new comic, who had brought in more than 15 people, until late in the game. That way, all of his fans would be forced to stick around, drinking and eating, until he came on stage. No need to send a large chunk of his audience home early because you put their guy on too early.

I ended the evening with Margie, bringing up the rear. She had dressed up in a polka-dotted shift that looked ridiculous on her masculine frame. But that was the whole point. The crowd, that part of the crowd that was still there, laughed themselves silly, mostly because of her outfit.

I felt sorry for her in a way, watching her dress up like that, just to get a laugh, like Anthony Quinn in *Requiem for a Heavyweight*, a once proud boxer reduced to dressing up like an Indian to make it on the pro wrestling circuit. But Margie didn't seem to mind. She actually seemed to be enjoying herself immensely.

And Dylan thought she was the bomb. He was smiling like crazy in the corner, leaning up against his broom, just like I do when I'm working at *Trader Joe's*. Mona had let him keep his job as clean-up boy. Sweet.

Mona gave me a couple of pointers after the show, like I should never, ever, MC again, and that I had wasted the newbie kid by putting him in the wrong place in the rotation. He should have been at the end. She also said that I needed to lose Margie and come up with a kick-ass follow-up act to Sly's. I knew that a certain amount of her criticism was valid, but a lot of it was posturing. I could tell that deep down, she was really happy with the job I had done.

We had taken in $750 and after paying everybody, we had $600 for ourselves -- $400 for Mona, $200 for me. Not a fortune, but a start.

I was away. I was officially in the entertainment business. A playa!

Chapter Twenty-Two

Margie wasn't talking to me. She was livid.

I knew it had been a bonehead move. Let's face it. I had been around long enough to know that you are not supposed to sleep with the people you work with, kill skunks on your own doorstep. But I had been so lonely, and Daisy had been so willing, and it just sort of happened.

We had been flirting for years. That's just the kind of girl she was, Daisy. A dizzy, goofy, flirty blonde who had the sound judgment of a glue-sniffing twelve-year-old. She loved to have a good time, and didn't always think through the consequences.

It all happened kind of quickly, an accident really. It was after a couple of weeks of me running my own room at the club, and Daisy was rising to the occasion with each performance,

She was killing it every time now, and I was starting to see repeat customers which is rare, because people tend to only go to comedy shows every once in a while. Even people who love comedy shows a lot don't go all the time.

But I knew it wasn't the comedy shows that the guys were loving. I knew it was Daisy. I was starting to see three or four of them show up every Thursday night, packed in up in the front row, waiting for her turn to come out on stage. Frequently, they would either leave when she finished her act, and before the other comedians did their thing, or they stuck around until after the show to try to get her phone number. She would giggle and bat her eyelashes, but would never hand it out.

Because of all this success, Daisy was feeling good and I was feeling good, and before you knew it one thing led to another. We had a couple of drinks too many one night and we ended up in the sack. It was the first time I had made love since Lettie died. It was weird. Not bad, just weird.

I thought it was going to be really sensual and really exciting to make it with a pretty girl, and it was, kind of. But after you've made love to the same person for so long, and really loved making love to that person for so long, it's sort of sad, in a strange kind of way, when you make love to somebody else. It just doesn't feel right.

And of course, in the morning, we were both embarrassed, hung over and embarrassed. Daisy and I quickly realized that it was a mistake, that remaining friends and business colleagues was infinitely more important than bumping uglies. That's what Sly used to call it, bumping uglies.

Margie, naturally, was not pleased. She saw Daisy leaving the apartment building the next morning when she was coming in to take care of Dylan.

"You did it with Dylan in the other room!"

"He was asleep, Margie."

"I can't believe it," she sounded almost hurt. "I hope you and the little slut had a good time."

"Margie, Daisy is not a slut. Besides, it was a one-time thing."

"Oh right," Margie said. "Believe me, sluts never do it just one time."

She was obviously hurt.

"You almost sound jealous, Margie?"

"Oh don't be ridiculous," she said. "Don't flatter yourself."

Slosser took to teaching Dylan the ins and outs of filming and editing with a video cam. I thought it was really nice of Slosser to take my son under his wing, and Dylan loved it, of course, sitting back in the dark booth with Slosser during the shows, watching all the comics get up and show off their stuff.

Dylan was particularly fascinated with the timing mechanism on the camera, how long each comedian took to do his routine. It excited him to see if the comics could stay on their schedules, nail their timing and hit all their jokes and punch lines at just the right moment.

Comics usually get 10-15 minutes to perform at shows, although almost all of them try to stretch it out another minute or two to get extra time to try out new material.

My job, or Mona's, depending on the night, was to let the comics know when they had gone over their allotted time. We usually did this by holding up a cell phone and shining its light towards the stage. Sometimes, the comic saw it. Sometimes, he didn't. Sometimes, he just ignored it.

This was a whole lot better than the old system where flashing red lights, like the kind on an ambulance or a fire engine, were attached to the ceiling and swirled around in the back of the room, letting everyone, even the customers, know that the bit had gone on too long.

In the dark room, Slosser and Dylan didn't need cell phones or flashing lights. They knew what was going on up on the stage because of the timer graphic on the video. It told them second by second how long a comic was taking to do his routine.

Because of his photographic memory and because he had memorized almost every routine these guys had ever done, Dylan could tell if the comic was ahead or behind schedule.

"Sly's 14 seconds behind," he would whisper to Slosser. "And he only has two jokes to go."

It was like having a human egg timer by his side. Slosser would smile at Dylan and punch him gently in the arm. "Thataboy, Dylan, keep 'em honest. Keep 'em honest."

"So what's it like to be a woman?"

I couldn't believe I had just asked that question.

"What exactly do you mean?" Margie answered, hesitating, trying to figure out where I was going with this.

"I mean, how is it different now than from when you were a man?"

There was a long pause, so I added: "Look, we don't have to talk about this if you don't want to."

There was another long pause.

"Yeah," I said. "We'd better just drop it. Sorry, I brought it up."

"No, we can talk about it," Margie said. "I don't mind."

It had been several years since her sex change operation, and I had gotten pretty used to her high-pitched sing-song voice. But every once in a while, it would be like I was hearing it for the first time, and I would have to try real hard not to bust out laughing. It seemed so unnatural, that voice of hers, so squeaky, so freaky. Sometimes, I could swear that she was putting me on.

But I knew she wasn't. Say what you want about Margie, but she is as honest as the day is long. You wouldn't think that a hairy, Cro-Magnon-sized transgender female could be authentic, but if anyone is, Margie is. She is the real deal. With each passing day, I admire her candor and courage more and more.

"I think the biggest difference is the maternal and relationship components," Margie said. "I don't know if it's the hormone treatments or what, but both of those aspects of my personality seem to be much more volatile than they were before."

"Has you sense of humor changed at all?" I asked, unable to stay away from my favorite subject, humor and what makes people laugh.

"Interesting question," she said, pausing for a second to give it some serious consideration. "I'm not sure." And then added, "Some jokes that I used to find funny I don't find funny anymore."

"Like what?" I asked.

"Do you remember the one that went: *How can you trust something that bleeds for four days a month and still lives?* she asked.

"Yeah."

"Well, I don't like that one anymore," she said, grinning.

I burst out laughing. "Do you have a misandrist joke that's taken its place?"

Margie was surprised I knew what the word "misandrist" meant. Lettie, my Ivy Leaguer, had taught it me. But Margie was a smart cookie herself with a good education. She had gone to Vassar. She just didn't talk about it.

"I guess my new favorite joke is probably: '*What's that useless, fleshy part around the penis?"*

She paused.

"That would be the man."

I had heard it before, but I laughed anyway. Good jokes keep on giving.

"Actually," Margie continued. "I love men. That's why I changed genders."

This was the first time we had ever discussed her sexual preference. We had talked about her sex change operation until we were blue in the face, but we had never actually discussed her preference for men.

Margie poured herself another glass of red wine, and kicked back on the sofa, stretching out her mammoth body like a python uncoiling in the noon-day sun.

"In hindsight, are you glad you did it?" I asked. "Are you glad you got the operation?"

She looked at me through dewy eyes.

"I didn't have a choice, Lance," she said sweetly. "I had to do it. It's who I am."

I was immensely grateful that Margie hadn't brought up Daisy all night. It was a sore spot and I knew how angry Margie had been when she found out. Instead the evening was very enjoyable, quite pleasant really.

.

We joked around a little bit more, and then Margie said she had to go home. It was getting late. She had to be at work early for her telemarketing job.

"I had a great time," she said. "It was nice to spend time together, just the two of us."

“Yes, it was,” I conceded.

Dylan was sleeping over at a new friend’s house, a new friend that he had made at his new school. For a second, I had a bizarre feeling that Margie was hanging on, waiting for me to say something else, waiting for me to make a move of some kind.

But then, she grabbed her coat, held open the door, and said goodbye.

Mona was finding new ways to use young Dylan. When she found out about his photographic memory and his human calculating machine of a brain, she started letting him collect cover charges. One, he was good at it. Two, he could be trusted with the cash and would hand it over to her whenever she saw him. And three, at any point during the evening, she could bump into him and find out where the money stood.

"$850 gross," he would say, "Minus $250 in expenses, leaves you with $600 net. Best Friday you've had since Sept. 27 when you had $925 gross, $655 profit."

Mona got the biggest kick out of this, having a walking, talking cash register sidekick that she could pose a financial question to anytime she wanted, and get back a quick, accurate and precise download.

Like most things, you couldn't tell whether Dylan liked this part of his job or not, whether he was having fun, or just putting in the hours. His emotions never showed. But what you could tell was that he was proud of it, that he really liked the idea of having a job, having something that made him look like he was a normal young man, and not just some freak hanger-on at the club.

Mona still wasn't paying him, at least not with a paycheck. But I had a sneaking suspicion that she was slipping him some cash on the side. If she was, it was piling up somewhere back at the apartment, because Dylan just didn't give two shits about money.

I smiled. You could get Dylan to count it up for you, but you couldn't make him worship it, not like the rest of us. Not a material bone in his body.

They were doing something pretty cool at Dylan's school. They were planning to put on a play written, directed, and acted entirely by autistic people.

Each actor would write his own mini-play, a kind of play within a play, describing what it was like to be autistic, what it was like trying to live in a world full of straight people. They were thinking of calling it "The Autism Monologues" and they were bringing in a big name director, who had an autistic nephew. He was donating his time to pull the play together.

Naturally, Dylan was dying to be part of the cast, having caught the stage bug from watching all the comedians do their thing. I encouraged him to try out. I couldn't wait to see what he was going to come up with for his piece.

Chapter Twenty-Three

"I'll see your 25 cents and bump you a dime."

It was the Monday night poker game. Monday was a good night to play poker because it was a shit night to run a comedy room. Nobody goes out on Mondays.

We had no business playing poker for money, broke as we all were, except for Roscoe, but it allowed us to get together outside work and talk trash, which was one of our favorite things to do. And we were only playing for a couple of bucks a hand anyway.

"You seeing Donnelly much these days?" Roscoe wanted to know.

"Some, but not as much as I used to," I said. "We're not on the same shift anymore at work."

"I thought he'd be here," Roscoe said.

I shrugged. "He was invited."

"I'll see your dime," Sly said, peering deeply into his hand. He'd been quiet all night for some reason. Usually, he was the big mouth on Poker Night.

"What's up with you tonight, Sly?" Roscoe wanted to know.

"Nothing," Sly said, giving him a cold, even stare.

"Just asking," Roscoe returned.

"What's new with you?" I asked Slosser, trying to steer the conversation away from Sly, who clearly had something bothering him.

“Not much,” he said. “Having a tough time with my landlord right now. He’s giving me a lot of shit about my rent.”

“How so?”

“Well, I’ve fallen a couple of months behind recently and he’s super pissed off.”

Everyone stopped talking for a while, while we all looked at our hands. Roscoe had a pair of queens showing and we were all trying to figure out if we could beat him. Naturally, nobody was giving anything away about what was in their hands, at least not by their expressions.

“How you doing with that video cam business of yours?” Roscoe asked.

“Not great,” said Slosser. “A lot of the new guys don’t want to be filmed. They think they can figure out this comedy business all by themselves."

This was a little bit of a shot at Roscoe who had steadfastly refused to use a camera for help ever since he had come into the rooms. I wouldn't be caught dead without the videotape. It was the only feedback system I had for improving my performance, except, of course, for Dylan and Margie.

"Yeah," Slosser said. "It's a tough way to make a living. I don't know what to do, raise prices, start becoming more aggressive in my promotion, try to find more shows to work. But I have to do something. It's getting bad."

"Don't raise prices," I quipped.

But Slosser didn't laugh. He was not amused.

He charged $10 apiece per show to shoot a comic's performance. Not a lot of money, but then none of us comics made much money so he knew he couldn't raise his prices.

"Jesus," Sly said finally. "Can we just play poker for once? Do we always having to be talking business?"

Something was bothering Sly. Either that or he had a really terrible hand.

"She's what?"

"She's pregnant."

"Pregnant? Daisy's pregnant?"

"Yeah, BB, she's pregnant."

Jesus, I thought. This is not good. This is really not good.

I knew that this meant that Sly had been sleeping with Daisy, probably for a while. What Sly didn't know, and what Daisy wasn't about to tell him, was that I had had a one night stand with her as well.

Holy Shit. No wonder he was so distracted at the poker game.

"So what are you going to do, man?"

'I don't know," Sly said. "I've got to think it through."

"What a bummer," I said. "Do you want to keep it? The kid, I mean?"

"I don't know, dude."

I paused a second and then asked. "Do you love her?"

I couldn't help it. For some reason, I needed to know.

"Of course, I love Daisy," Sly said.

My heart stopped. Shit.

"We all love Daisy. I'm just not sure if I love her in that way, if you know what I mean," Sly added.

I started to breathe again.

"Yeah, man," I said glumly. "I know exactly what you mean."

I wished I could have thought of something clever to say, but I couldn't. There's no such thing as a good joke when a woman comes between two friends. No such thing.

Chapter Twenty-Four

The line-up had pretty much taken shape by this point. I was in the groove and I didn't feel like I needed to change it every night.

I had come up with Sammy as my MC. Sammy had been around a few years, done a bunch of lower level television shows, was not a superstar, but was competent, and very, very high energy, which was just what you need in an MC, somebody who can pump up the crowd from the get-go.

The only thing you had to watch with Sammy was that he didn't get too much into the nose candy before or during the show. If he came with cocaine in him, or on him, he could start revving too high and the whole delicate mechanism of being an MC could unravel quickly, really quickly.

Timing is everything in comedy and cocaine messes with timing real bad. It speeds you up, and once the audience turns on you because your timing's off, it can make you angry, which, in turn, makes the audience even more hostile. It can become a vicious downward spiral.

But Sammy had been being a good boy lately. If he was doing any drugs, he was doing them after the show.

My number one slot was going to Judy most nights. She was a solid, no nonsense comedian who told jokes about her husband and her kids. What made her shtick work was that she looked so straight. She would surprise the audience when she came out with her dirty girl punch lines in between her soiled diaper, burning dinner, and lumpy husband set-ups.

The next performer was Jake, who was pretty damn funny. Most gay guys in comedy tend to be flashy, flaunt their sexuality. Jake was as gay as the day is long, but he was soft spoken and unassuming with a gentle sense of humor. He didn't focus on his sexuality, choosing instead to lean toward intellectual, philosophical stuff. He was a big hit with women, and of course, his gay brethren. He was also easy on the eyes to both genders.

Daisy, who wasn't even close to showing yet, was in her usual spot and still knocking it out of the park every night. She was living the life. Everything in her world seemed to be going great. I guess she really wanted to be pregnant.

Roscoe was comfortable following her. Not too early in the evening. Not too late.

I left the middle-of-the-lineup, the headliner spot, to Sly, who, until recently, had been killing audiences. They probably didn't even notice that he had changed. But I could tell he was just going through the motions, mailing it in.

I kept the next slot open for a newcomer, usually a different one every few weeks or so. Their job was to bring in friends and family who paid enough in cover charges and drink orders to keep the rest of my troupe in business.

By placing the newbie late in the evening, I could guarantee that his friends wouldn't leave before their buddy came on. Sadly, most of these new guys, the overwhelming majority of these new guys, would only play two or three shows and then they would be gone forever. Once all their friends had come to see them a couple of times, they would stop coming. And then the comics couldn't generate enough bums in seats anymore, and they would have to be cut from the roster.

I tried to console myself when this happened, when I had to cut one of them, by remembering that if it weren't for me, they wouldn't have ever seen the limelight at all; they would never have had a chance to pursue their dreams in the first place. But it was small solace. The truth was this business could really be brutal.

After the last joke was told and the night was over, Dylan would do his thing, picking up all the cups and bottles, taking them into the dish washer, then sweeping and mopping up the joint, before heading home with me.

For the first time, since Lettie had passed, I was feeling like life might actually have some potential.

Sure, Daisy was pregnant, and sure I was going to have to talk to Sly at some point, probably pretty soon. But Dylan had a job and was doing well at his new school; my Thursday night room was humming along, not as spectacularly as I would like, but not bad at all; and I had a host of good friends, really good friends, people I could count on.

"You don't want me to talk to him?"

"No."

"But we have to tell him."

"No we don't."

"Aw c'mon, Daisy. You can't let the guy think he's the father if he's not."

"He is the father."

"You don't know that."

"Yes, I do."

"How?"

"I just do."

Poor Daisy. Poor thing.

"Look," she said. "I know all you guys think I'm just some ditzy bitch who's easy, who will spread her legs for anyone. Well, it's not true. You probably won't believe it, but I've only had sex with two people in the past year – you and Sly. And frankly, you were a big mistake."

That hurt.

"I'm not blaming you," she said. "It takes two to tango, but I sure wish it hadn't happened. Now, look at the mess we're in."

I didn't know what to say. I just sat there like a bump on the proverbial log.

She kept going.

"BB, I think I might love Sly. In fact, I do love Sly. He means the world to me. I think we have a real shot at happiness. I just don't want to blow it before we even get started. I don't want him to go ballistic when he finds out that you and I slept together. I would be devastated if I lost him."

I looked at her closely. She was so sincere, so sweet, so tender and loving, in so many ways. Sly could do a lot worse.

But I had to be honest with her.

"Daisy, you can't start a new life with dishonesty. I know that's easy for me to say. I'm not the one who's pregnant. I'm not the one in love. But I just think you should give this a lot of thought. And you need to give it a lot of thought very quickly. Sly needs some answers and I imagine, you'll start showing soon. This isn't something you can finesse."

"I know," she said softly.

"Besides, it's all going to come out eventually," I continued. "I'm white. Sly's black. That baby's going to be one color or the other. There's just no hiding that. It's something we are going to have to deal with. But I think you should probably go and get tested before you do anything else. Go and find out who the father is. Now."

Chapter Twenty-Five

Everybody pretty much has to have a job on the side. Most of the comics can't make it on comedy alone.

Margie has a telemarketing gig, which is perfect because no one can see her over the phone, and even though she has a high, squeaky voice, she is very competent and very sympathetic with callers. It's a nice fit, her job.

Daisy is a hostess at TGIF's, another perfect match, she being all airy fairy and such. I wondered if TGIF had some policy on preggie women being hostesses. I wondered if they would make her quit or take leave when she started showing. Either way, I hoped they would keep paying her.

Roscoe, oddly enough, is actually pretty successful. He runs his own advertising agency during the day. It isn't a huge company, but it does fairly well. He only does comedy because he loves it so much.

Slosser has a shit job, a job he hates. He is a toll-taker at the Triborough Bridge, which they have recently re-named The Robert F. Kennedy Bridge, a name no one is ever going to use. It will always be the Triborough to anyone who lives in New York. It sounded like the worst job in the world.

And Sly sells cars, used cars, mostly Toyotas, which wasn't all that bad until the Japanese car maker had a massive recall recently. Then business headed south for a while. Not great news when you're trying to figure out if you want to be a father or not.

"What's going on in the great wide world of comedy?" Donnelly asked when I showed up for work one day. Even though we worked in the same place, we were working different hours now, so we didn't get to see each other all that much. "Still living the dream?"

"It's not bad," I said. "I'm having fun running my own show. You'll have to come see it sometime."

Donnelly, decked out in his usual red flannel shirt and blue jeans, nodded.

For some reason, I was having a hard time getting to that place where best friends hang out, where they can anticipate each other's next sentence and flawlessly predict their pal's next move.

"Listen," I said, going for broke. "I need to ask you some questions, bounce some ideas off you."

"Shoot," Donnelly said, without committing to anything.

So I laid out the whole thing for him, the whole ball of wax. I told him about the one-night stand with Daisy, her being pregnant, about she and Sly being an item, about me not talking to Sly and Daisy wanting to keep it a secret from Sly forever.

"Well, buddy," Donnelly said at long last. "That's a deep hole you've dug yourself."

"Yeah, it kind of is," I said. "I wish I knew what to do."

Donnelly gave me the look guys give each other when they are basically telling their buddy: I am so glad I'm not in your shoes.

"It's a tough one," Donnelly said, finally. "You don't want to break the two of them up, Sly and Daisy. On the other hand, what if you are the father of that kid, what are you going to do then?"

"Have the kid," I said, without missing a beat. "Of course, I would have the kid."

"Does Daisy know that? Did you tell her that? I mean she's the one who actually has to have the kid."

"No," I said, "I haven't gotten that far yet."

"When did you plan on telling her?"

"I don't know."

"You are kind of laying the whole thing on her, aren't you?" Donnelly said, without recrimination. "You told her to go to the doctor to find out who the father is and then you told her that you weren't sure if you could withhold the truth from Sly. You sure are putting a lot of weight on that poor girl's shoulders."

I hadn't even thought of it that way. I had only been thinking about it from my point of view, my relationship with her, my relationship with Sly, my relationship with a possible offspring. But I hadn't really considered what it must be like from Daisy's vantage point.

Poor thing, she must really be struggling with all of this, even though she appeared to be happier lately than I had ever seen her. I wondered if she had just been putting on a good front. I wondered if she was falling apart on the inside.

"Another thing," Donnelly said. "Have you thought about how this is going to affect Dylan? How do you think he's going to react if that baby turns out to be yours? How do you think sharing his Dad is going to sit with him?"

Once again, I realized I had only been thinking about myself, not the possibility of Dylan having a sibling. Donnelly, as usual, was cutting to the chase.

"And Lance?" he said, rubbing his hands through his thick red mop.

"Yeah."

"It's none of my business, but there is someone else to consider," Donnelly said.

"Who?"

"Margie."

"Margie?"

"Yeah. Margie. She's crazy nuts about you."

Mona was talking to a cop.

“What’s up?” I said as I approached them.

“There have been a string of burglaries in the neighborhood recently,” Mona said, motioning towards the policeman. “The officer here was just asking me if we’d seen anything unusual lately.”

“I haven’t seen anything,” I said. “Who got robbed?”

“The bodega across the way and the ice cream parlor down the street. Small jobs, nothing big,” the policeman said.

“Do you have a description of the guy?” Mona asked, and then added as an after-thought. “Or gal?”

“No,” said the officer, “Other than the perpetrator wore a ski mask and a bulky black jacket. And we are pretty sure it is a man.”

"Do you think this person is dangerous?" I asked.

"Hard to tell," said the policeman. "He always threatens the person behind the counter with a gun, but no one has actually seen a gun yet. He may just be sticking his finger out inside the jacket, pretending like he's got one."

"Well, listen," Mona said. "We'll definitely keep an eye out and let you know if we see anything."

"Thanks," said the officer. "Appreciate that."

"No worries," I said.

But actually I was worried. I was suddenly worried about the neighborhood, something I had never considered before. Suddenly, I was worried about Dylan and his safety. I knew it didn't make any sense. I was with my son almost all of the time when I was at the club. But there was still something unsettling about this burglary business that bothered me deeply.

I tracked Daisy down at TGIF.

“Can we talk?” I asked.

“About what?” she said, knowing full well what it was about.

“About the baby,” I said. “It’s important.”

I wasn’t dying to have this conversation, but I could still hear Donnelly’s words ringing in my ears. I was trying, in my own way, to make amends to Daisy for my earlier selfish behavior.

“Yeah, sure,” she said, unconvincingly. “Let’s go in the back and talk. It’s quieter there.”

When we got back in the storage area, I just blurted it out, "Listen, Daisy, it's important for you to know that you don't have to go through this thing alone. I think you should have the baby and, if the baby's mine, I'm willing to help out. I'm prepared to step up and meet my responsibilities."

"Is this a proposal of marriage?" Daisy asked, letting the thought hang in the air for a moment.

When I didn't come back with a snappy answer, she grabbed me by the arm and shook me.

"I was just kidding you?" she said. "I don't want to marry you."

I was relieved and hurt at the same time.

"Do you want to have the baby?" I asked.

"Of course, I do. I want to have the baby and I want to have it

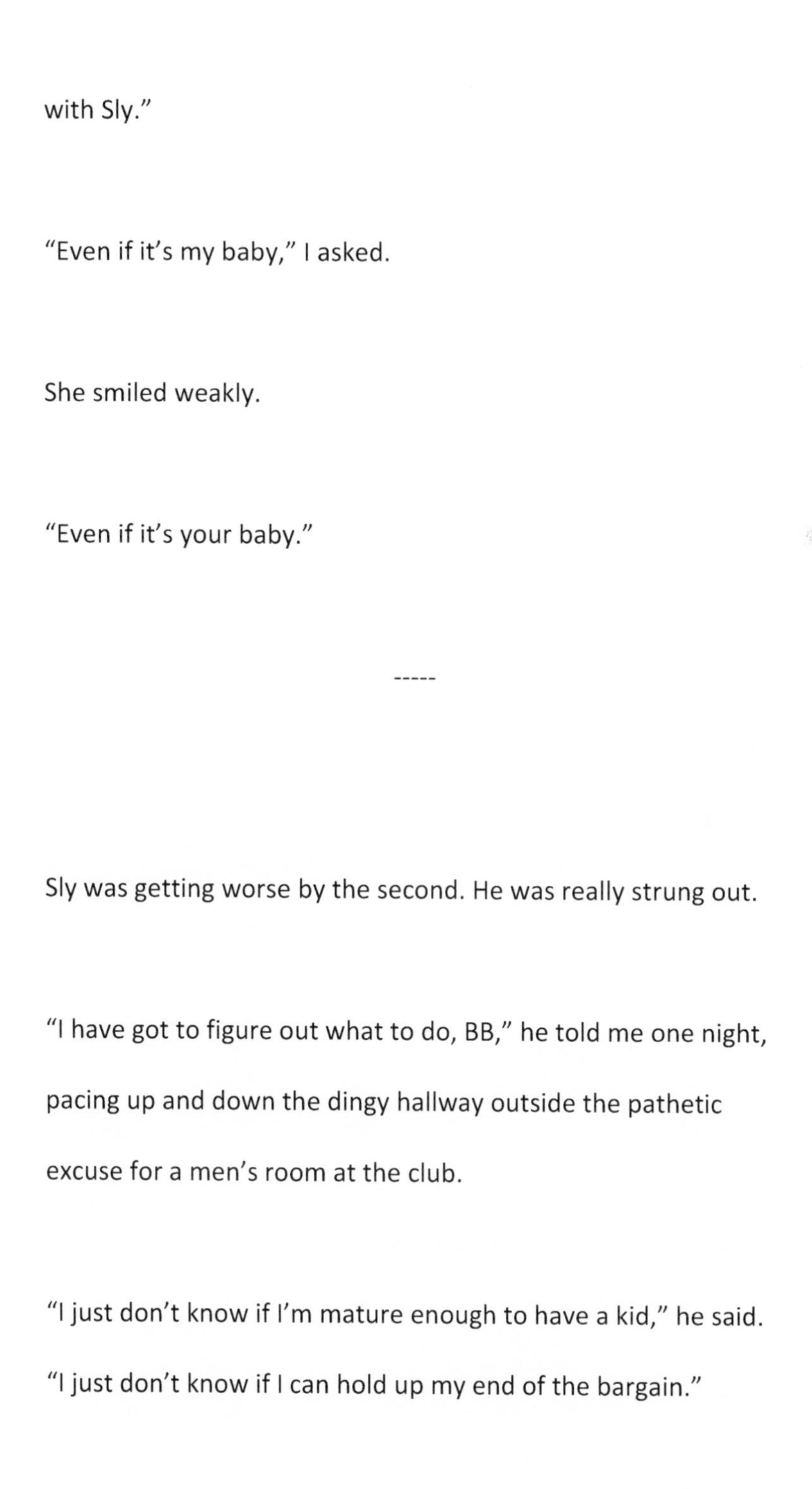

with Sly."

"Even if it's my baby," I asked.

She smiled weakly.

"Even if it's your baby."

Sly was getting worse by the second. He was really strung out.

"I have got to figure out what to do, BB," he told me one night, pacing up and down the dingy hallway outside the pathetic excuse for a men's room at the club.

"I just don't know if I'm mature enough to have a kid," he said. "I just don't know if I can hold up my end of the bargain."

"Look, man," I said. "If I can do it, you can do it."

Sly stop and inspected me, like I was some specimen in the insect house at the zoo.

"Do you like being a father?" he asked.

"I love it, Sly. It's the most important thing to me in the world," I said.

"You love it, even though..." he stopped and didn't say it.

"Even though what, Sly? Even though I have an autistic son? Is that what you meant?"

He just looked at me. I stared back.

"Yeah, I guess so," Sly said. "I guess that's what I meant."

We continued to stare at each other.

And then, Sly said, “I guess what I want to know, and you know I love you to death BB and would do anything for you, I guess what I want to know is: would you do it all over again if you could? I mean you’ve had a pretty rotten go of it, haven’t you? Knowing what you know now, would you get married again, would you have a kid again? What would you do in my shoes?”

Sly had hit me right where it hurt. I hadn’t even contemplated this question before. Would I have married Lettie again, knowing that she would die so tragically and so incredibly young? Would I have fathered Dylan again, knowing that he would be autistic and have such a difficult time fitting into the world?

Heavy, heavy questions.

And then I looked Sly in the eye and laid it on him as

convincingly as I possibly could.

"Yeah, Sly, I would. I would do it all over again... in a heartbeat."

"We don't need for Sly to take a blood test," Daisy said, "We just need to get one of his hairs or something, where they can get some of his DNA."

I nodded my head in acknowledgement.

"We can also do the test now. I'm eight weeks pregnant and my doctor says that should be enough time to get good results and not damage the baby," she said. "The bad news is that the results won't come in for another four-to-six weeks."

I nodded again. And then she said exactly what I was thinking,

"I'll be showing by then."

"Yep," I thought to myself.

This all meant that we couldn't do the test in time to give Sly a choice. If he decided that he didn't want to have the kid, because, for example, he found out it was mine, it would be too late to decide on an abortion.

Daisy knew just where my head was at.

"I'm having the baby no matter what," she said. "With or without Sly."

"Does he know?"

"Yep," she said. "I told him yesterday."

"Whoa," I said. "How did he take it?"

She just stared at me.

"Okay," she said softly, her eyes starting to mist. "He took it okay."

I knew enough not to pursue the subject any further. Jesus, what a mess we've made, I thought. God only knows how we'll dig our way out of this hole.

"Another place got hit last night," Mona said. "Someone picked the lock on the hardware store and broke in and emptied the cash register drawer."

"Wow," I said. "Why do you suppose the guy keeps hitting on the same neighborhood. Doesn't he think he'll get caught eventually?"

“I don’t know,” she said, “but the cops were around again today, asking a lot of questions about who works here and if anybody’s having serious money or drug problems.”

“Oh great,” I said. “That really narrows down the list of suspects. We all have money problems.”

Chapter Twenty-Six

I was dying to tell Margie about the Daisy situation because I knew Daisy would be showing soon and when she did, Margie was going to be all over me with questions, not so nice questions.

Daisy still hadn't told Sly about our one-night peccadillo. She was waiting for him to come up with his decision, waiting for him to decide whether he was going to be a father, a father/husband combo, or none of the above.

The tension was starting to take its toll on me and, apparently, on Sly. Dylan told me that the black comedian's timing was way off, that he could see on videotape in the booth that Sly wasn't hitting his punch lines at even close to the right times.

And Daisy was finally showing signs that the strain was taking hold of her as well. It didn't matter how many guys were sitting in the front row, staring at her, she was starting to get worn down by the baby drama, the baby drama that only she and I knew about, the baby drama where I might be the father.

To add to my worries, the Thursday night room had started to lose its luster. I didn't know if it was because the patrons had seen all of the acts before and were kind of worn out by the same cast. I didn't think that was the case because I had a pretty steady stream of newbies coming through, bringing with them fresh material and fresh cover charges and two-drink minimums. Mona and I also used to do our bits every once in a while if there was time or someone didn't show. That should have provided some variety as well.

But whatever the reason, I was starting to feel the pinch financially and I was sure Mona and the others were too.

Without warning and much to my surprise, Dylan suddenly had a girlfriend. At least, that's what Margie told me when I got home from my daily, mid-morning jog. She said my son was madly, passionately in love with some girl named Suzanne whom he had met down at his new school.

I was in shock. I thought Dylan might actually go through his entire life without ever falling in love. And madly? Passionately? Margie had a tendency to exaggerate.

When I heard the news, I was initially thrilled, and then, as my naturally neurotic mind started kicking into gear, I started worrying about Dylan, about how an autistic kid would handle love and, possibly sex, at some point.

Look at me, I thought, I'm 39 and, as recent events suggest, I can't even keep my own wiener in my trousers. What the hell is he going to do with those kinds of urges?

"Mommy says that you have been seeing this girl..." I started to say to Dylan, before pulling up short.

Mommy? Where the hell did that come from?

"Margie says," I started over, "that there's a girl that you like at your school."

"She's really great. She's a good person," Dylan said, matter-of-factly, adding: "She's my girlfriend. I love her."

The voice sounded like Dylan, but the language sounded like it was coming from someone from Mars. I had never heard him talk like this before, at least not about a girl.

"Well, when did you meet her?" I asked, a little shocked by Dylan's confession of love.

"About two weeks ago," Dylan said. "On Tuesday Oct. 14 at 3:30 p.m. in the hallway at my school."

"Well, how do you know that she's your girlfriend?" I asked.

"She told me so," Dylan said without expression.

"She told you so?"

"Yes, she told me that we were in love and that we should be boyfriend and girlfriend," he said.

"And that's okay with you?"

"Yes, Dad. It's okay with me. In fact, it's great with me. We love each other. It's nice to have a girlfriend."

Margie was standing over in the corner, beaming away. I guessed she was entitled. After all, she was the one who taught him about the birds and the bees.

I was also wondering if she had heard my Freudian slip, my reference to her being Dylan's mother, and if so, what she thought of it.

I had to hand it to him. Sly had stepped up big time.

"I've asked Daisy to move in with me," Sly said. "I'm not sure I can get married yet, but I do care for her and I'm not going to let her have that baby alone."

It was the right thing to do from my perspective, and I was proud of my friend for doing it. But I was still feeling like the world's biggest heel. If that kid turned out to be mine, there was going to be hell to pay. I thought Sly might even try to kill me. I could see the headline. "Angry Black Man Slays Cheating White Man". And everybody would say Sly had every right to do it. And they would be right.

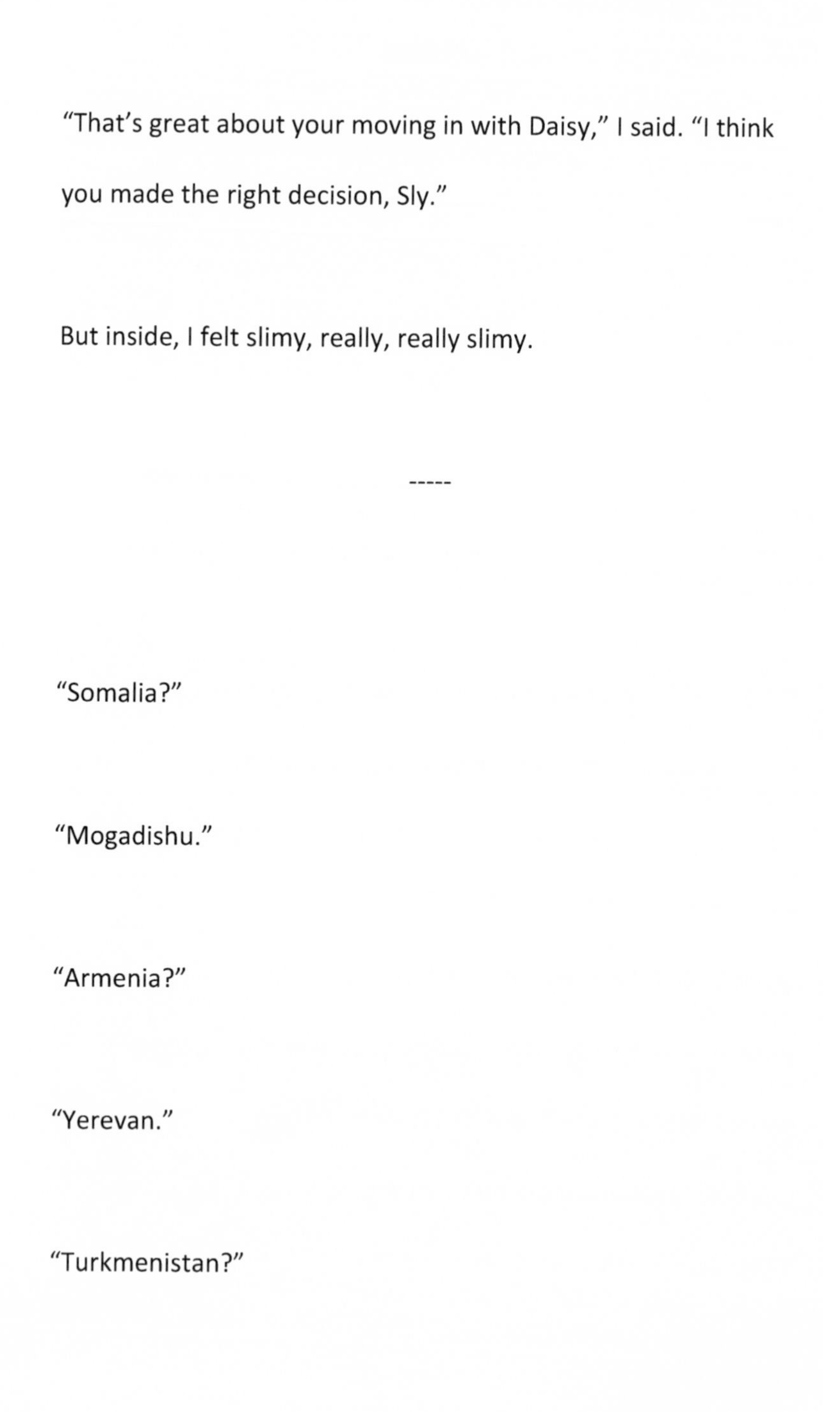

"That's great about your moving in with Daisy," I said. "I think you made the right decision, Sly."

But inside, I felt slimy, really, really slimy.

"Somalia?"

"Mogadishu."

"Armenia?"

"Yerevan."

"Turkmenistan?"

"Ashgabat."

"Brunei?"

"Bandar Seri Begawan."

God, he was good. I didn't know half of these places were countries, much less what the names of their capitals were.

Margie was testing Dylan, seeing if he had retained all the knowledge that he had picked up about world capitals all those years ago when Lettie first bought him the talking globe.

Dylan hadn't lost any of it, as far as I could tell. It was all stored someplace in that remarkable brain of his. It suddenly occurred to me that if I had had any sense I would have gotten Dylan on the TV trivia show *Jeopardy* years ago. We'd be filthy rich by now.

Watching the two of them – Margie and Dylan -- was like watching a really, good tennis player hit a ball against a wall. As long as she kept feeding him questions, he was always going to keep hitting nice returns, keep coming up with the right answers.

It was so heart-warming to see them together. They got on so well. It may have been a weird, little family scene we had going on, the transgender caretaker and the autistic boy, but it was my family scene. And I loved it.

Chapter Twenty-Seven

It was quite a moving-in party. Pretty much everybody turned out to lend a hand.

Sly had a small apartment on the Lower East Side, which was just going to be big enough for the both of them. Who knew what was going to happen when the baby came along?

Daisy was giving up the tiniest efficiency I had ever seen, down in Chelsea. She was over the moon to be moving into Sly's place, even if they weren't getting married right away, if ever. I guessed she was taking this one step at a time.

"It's got its own kitchen... in a separate room," she squealed, like she was divulging the most incredible luxury feature ever.

Even Roscoe showed up to help out. Everyone thought beforehand that he was going to be really useful because he was the largest, bulkiest guy in the group, and had obviously lifted weights at some point in his life. But it turned out that he had been a CEO for a little bit too long. He wasn't into heavy lifting. He was more into telling all the rest of us what to do, where to put the stuff, how to pick up large objects without hurting ourselves, things like that.

Sly seemed a little shell-shocked by the whole proceeding. But he was holding up well and putting on a brave face. I didn't think he had any idea how much stuff Daisy had crammed into her little Chelsea studio or how it was all going to fit into his one-bedroom pad.

Sly also appeared a little concerned that Margie and Daisy were spending so much time discussing what kind of curtains were needed in the kitchen and, how, by getting rid of a few things here and there, and by buying a few other things on sale, "you might just be able to turn this place into something adorable." Sly frowned. He was not all that big on adorable.

But everybody else was having a blast, hauling all of Daisy's junk up three flights of stairs to Sly's apartment. There was a lot of laughing and joke-telling, as we tried to get different pieces of furniture around the bends in the awkward, paint-chipped stairwell.

Dylan was busy, the whole time, keeping track of how everyone was doing.

"You're thirty-eight percent of the way through," he said with his usual deadpan. "You should be all done by 2:37 p.m. if you keep up this pace."

That, in and of itself, made everyone laugh -- Conductor Dylan and his Mussolini Express.

"Don't beat us, Massah Dylan," Sly said, with a grin.

"Thataboy, Dylan," Mona threw in. "Keep the trains a'running."

But our little group didn't actually keep up with Dylan's anticipated pace, probably because we started drinking beer and smoking herb. But we wrapped up around 5 o'clock, in time for everyone to have a few hours off before that night's show.

"Thanks, everyone," Sly said at the end of the move, putting his arm around a beaming Daisy. "You are the best friends a guy could have."

"That's a sad state of affairs," Slosser quipped, as everyone began gathering up their things to leave.

It had been a good day, getting the whole gang together, and helping Sly and Daisy move in, even if no one but Sly, Daisy and I knew about the baby, even if Sly didn't know that the baby might not be his.

For some inexplicable reason, the robberies just stopped. I thought it might have been because the cops were starting to get much more aggressive in trying to find the guy who was doing them.

At one point or another, they had hauled all of the troupe in for questioning, all of us -- Mona, Slosser, Daisy, Sly, me, the lot, everyone except for Roscoe. I guessed they thought he didn't need the money or something.

The cops even tried to question Dylan. Where was he when he wasn't taking tickets and counting the money? Did he ever leave the club during the middle of the show? Stuff like that. I was furious, of course. I didn't do myself any favors when I told the cops pointedly to lay off Dylan.

But Dylan himself kind of liked having the officers ask him questions. He loved accounting for his whereabouts in a very precise way.

"From 6:53 p.m. until 9:27 p.m., I was at The Big Apple Comedy Club," he told the cops. "I took tickets for 29 minutes, picked up cups and glasses for 13 minutes and swept up and mopped up for 31 minutes. The rest of the time -- 21 minutes -- I was in the booth looking at videotapes of the performances. I saw four performances."

The police officer who was questioning him was a little taken aback. "You're very exact, aren't you?" he said. The cop thought that Dylan might be pulling his chain, making fun of him.

"He's autistic," I said. "It's just the way he sees the world."

"I can draw you a map of where I was all night if you would like that," Dylan told the officer, without changing expression.

"No, that's alright, kid," the policeman said, finally relenting, finally realizing that this young man had special talents, and robbery probably wasn't one of them.

The questioning of Mona, Sly, Daisy, Slosser, me and some of the others did not go particularly well, primarily because we all had motives for needing cash. All of us, to one degree or another, were slowly going, or were already, broke.

But we all had alibis too. We could all honestly say that we were in the club at the time of the robberies on Thursday nights. Oh sure, Sly would sneak out for a cigarette every once in a while; Daisy would go for a short stroll after her gig before she came back to watch everyone else; and I was known to go out for a slice of pizza on occasion. But by and large, all of us could say, hand on heart, that we had spent the night with each other, in the club, doing comedy.

I didn't think any of us seriously thought that anyone else in our clan was guilty of robbery, but we were all relieved when the robberies suddenly stopped. It was just one less strain to cope with in our already stressful lives.

Chapter Twenty-Eight

When Daisy lost the baby, I would like to say that I felt terrible for her and Sly, and I did, in a way. But the honest to God truth is that I was hugely relieved.

I would not have to confront Sly or Margie, two conversations I had been dreading having for weeks. And in a weird way, as it turns out, the loss of the child actually seemed to bring Sly and Daisy closer together.

They both went through hell short-term, but sometimes, when a couple has to face adversity together, it actually makes them stronger.

And that was the case here. Sly did not appear to feel like he had been tricked or gypped out of his bachelorhood, didn't feel like he had been set up by Daisy or anything. No, Sly ultimately decided that he and Daisy were good together, that maybe he should try to take their relationship to the next level, to give her all the help she needed as she grieved for her lost child.

And of course, Sly thought all along it was his kid. And who knows? There was a pretty good chance it was.

Naturally, Daisy had to take a couple of weeks off to recoup, not necessarily physically, but mentally and emotionally as much as anything. Fortunately, Guillermo, the affable Latino who used to hand out comedy show fliers, had a great delivery and was available and more than willing and able to fill in.

Most of the time, being a comic is a solo and competitive sport. You wouldn't think that we would be very good as team players. And the truth is, we usually aren't. In fact, we're usually horrible as team players.

But every once in a while, like this time, when Daisy lost her baby, the whole group actually showed that we could pull it together when we had to, and act like civilized grown-ups, pull it together and do what was needed to be done to protect one of our tribe.

"Why don't we live together?" she said. I almost blew my entire ham and cheese sandwich out my left nostril. I thought she was going to have to give me the Heimlich maneuver, I was choking so badly.

"I mean seriously, we could both save a lot of money," Margie said, after she had pounded on my back. "I'm already over at your place all the time anyway, looking after Dylan. Wouldn't it just make more sense if I was there full-time?"

Initially, I rejected Margie's suggestion out of hand. Things were just too chaotic to consider radical change at this point in time. But some months later, after the miscarriage, and as my financial situation at the Thursday night comedy session continued to deteriorate, I started to reconsider.

It would require Dylan and me moving into the same room, but it would also cut our living expenses by almost half. And of course, Dylan would be delighted. He was mad about Margie and would love to have her around full-time.

It took me awhile, but once I got my head around the concept, I was good to go. It actually made sense in a weird kind of way.

Dylan wanted me to meet Suzanne's parents. Great.

I knew from personal experience that all parents of autistic kids are used to some pretty intense bumps on the plane ride of life, but the Margie/Dylan/Lance home set-up was going to be off the charts by any standards.

"It's important to me, Dad," Dylan said. "I'm in love with Suzanne and we've been going out for 78 days. It's time you met her family. There are four of them, including her. Her Mom, her Dad and her brother. His name is Bobby, short for Robert."

Dylan and his details.

When Dylan insisted that Margie come along too, I started dancing the perverbial soft shoe, trying to figure out how to appease my son without getting into any kind of trouble. But I was having a helluva time seeing how this was going to play out in any way other than as a major disaster.

"Oh hi, Mister and Missus Jacobsen. My name's Lance Bonner.

I'm Dylan's father. My wife died in a freak car accident a few years ago and I decided the best way to honor her memory and take care of our autistic son was to quit my job, become a full-time stand-up comic, and move in with a man who thinks he's a woman. Could you please pass the pretzels?"

But I knew this was desperately important to Dylan, and therefore it had to become desperately important to me. I had to make a go of it somehow. Suck it up and impress the hell out of Suzanne's parents.

Not since I had taken those comedy lessons with the Seinfeld writer in my bid to impress Lettie and win her heart, had I felt such pressure to learn a new skill in such a short period of time.

Upwards and onwards.

To tell the truth, Dylan had been transformed by his courtship of Suzanne.

Most teen-age boys unravel in the presence of teen-age girls, particularly their first love. I remember my adolescence was the nightmare to end all nightmares as far as my parents were concerned. When I met my first girlfriend, all hell broke loose. I started drinking, smoking, doing drugs and rebelling against authority.

Dylan, on the hand, became a model citizen when he started dating. He immediately decided that he needed to straighten up, which was kind of odd, because he had never done anything bad or wrong in his entire life.

But from his point of view, time was of the essence. He needed to become an adult overnight, get a paying job, and start preparing for a future of responsibility and commitment.

"I think I should start being a lot more mature, Dad," Dylan said with his usual surreal seriousness. "I've got to accept that it's time for me to start acting like a man, instead of a child."

"Dylan," I pointed out. "You're 15. You're supposed to be enjoying yourself. You're supposed to be giving your father a hard time. You're supposed to be experimenting with life."

"That's not the way I roll," he retorted. "I respect you immensely. And now, I want you to respect me."

Not the way I roll? Obviously, Dylan had been spending some time with Sly.

"Well, son," I said. "Those are very laudable goals. But you are already the coolest person I know. You don't need to impress me any more than you already have."

"Well, that's all well and good, Dad," Dylan said, without emotion. "But being cool and being respected are not the same thing. I want you to learn to respect me as a man."

Whoa. Who was this kid? Where did he come from? How could we possibly be related?

Chapter Twenty-Nine

Living with Margie turned out to be a pleasant surprise. Most of my experiences with women had required radical adjustments on my part, even with Letitia. But with Margie it was like sticking my toes into an old pair of well-worn moccasins. It couldn't have been more natural, more comfortable.

She didn't own many things -- in that regard she was still very much like a man -- and the move was a breeze. The three of us didn't even ask anyone to help us with it. Margie, Dylan and I pulled it off in a matter of hours.

When it was done, Dylan and I looked at each other. We had a new roommate.

The whole first week went off without a hitch.

Even though we only had one bathroom, there were no

uncomfortable "you left the top off of the toothpaste" or "you left the toilet seat up" moments. It was almost like Margie had lived with us her entire life. Plus, the things she did move in with, some of her modern art, and her kitchen utensils and cooking paraphernalia, turned out to be welcome additions.

"I love being here," Margie said, on her eighth day of camping out at Chez Bonner.

"We love having you," Dylan quickly added.

I didn't say a thing. I just looked at the two of them and felt a tremendous sense of warmth and well-being.

Life really is stranger than fiction, I kept repeating to myself. You can't make this stuff up.

Who knew?

It turned out that the "Autism Monologues," the play that Dylan was in, caught the fancy of a certain university president, who took it upon himself to go and raise money to take the show on the road.

Both Dylan and Suzanne, two years his senior, had parts in the play, and they were excited beyond comprehension at the possibility of being able to take their show to other parts of the Tri-State area – Connecticut, New Jersey and New York State.

First stop was a performing arts theater on the campus of the aforementioned university president's school, Rutgers. Then it was off to a handful of other undergraduate institutions and community colleges, before ending the summer at a small theater in the sea shore town of Cape May, New Jersey.

Dylan had already communicated to Mona, that he might miss a few nights of work in order to accommodate his new acting career. "I would think that I might miss 31.5 to 43 hours this spring and summer. But don't worry. I am more than willing to make up those hours at an appropriate time."

Suzanne continued to enchant. With long flowing brown hair and hazel eyes to match, she was a delight to the eye, but more importantly she was just the sort of serious, but gently feminine, creature that Dylan needed and desired most at this impressionable stage of his life.

She always called me by my proper first name, never the formal Mister Bonner, or the informal BB, but always Lance. She was a middle of the roader, just like Dylan. She did not rebel against the universe, like most adolescents do. She just accepted it, as is.

I could not have asked for a better girlfriend for my son. She was just perfect. And in all candor, so were her parents, Bud and Stella, real down-to-earth Pennsylvanians who had moved to New York City as a young couple for his job.

To my considerable surprise, my dreaded meeting with them went swimmingly. At the last second, Margie decided not to go. But it didn't matter. Apparently, Suzanne had told them all about Margie beforehand, or at least what she had learned about her from Dylan.

"So you're a comedian?" Suzanne's dad asked.

"Yeah," I responded

"Can you tell me one of your jokes? It doesn't have to be your whole routine. Just one of your funnier jokes."

"Sure," I said. "Oh, by the way, what do you do for a living?"

"I'm an accountant," Bud said.

"No kidding," I responded. "Can you do part of my tax return? You don't have to do the whole thing. Just do a line or two."

Bud cracked up. The two of us were going to get along just fine.

It occurred to me after our visit that when you have an autistic child, you learn to spot intolerance and prejudice pretty earlier on. You also learn to despise both, to bend over backwards to be as inclusive and loving as possible with all manner of people. Suzanne's family didn't think twice about the legitimacy of our family. They welcomed us in with open arms.

"So do you ever think about having sex with her?"

"What?"

"I said do you ever think about having sex with her?"

"Are you crazy?"

"No, I was just wondering. I mean she has female organs and all. I was just wondering if the thought ever crossed your mind."

Margie and Daisy were in the ladies' room. Sly and I were at the table in a Greek neighborhood restaurant near my apartment.

"You're creeping me out, Sly," I said.

"Why?" Sly said, "You guys are good buddies. You live together. Your son's crazy about her. And she's a woman. That's what you keep telling me. She's a woman. So I was just wondering if the sex thought ever crossed your mind."

"No, Sly. I haven't thought about it," I said, a little irritated by this line of questioning, even though I couldn't tell exactly why.

"Okay," Sly said, a little irritated himself. "Okay. Let's just drop it. Let's just go back to having a good time. Alright?"

"Cool," I said. "Let's just go back to having a good time."

Chapter Thirty

Comedy Central, the holy grail of comedy in America, had just put out a list of the top 100 comics of all time. The Top Ten were Richard Pryor, George Carlin, Lenny Bruce, Woody Allen, Chris Rock, Steve Martin, Rodney Dangerfield, Bill Cosby, Roseanne Barr and Eddie Murphy, in that order.

"That's a seriously good list," Sly was saying, pointing out proudly that the number one guy was black. "But how can anyone really say who the best comedian of all time is? How can you rank them?"

"I agree," I said. "Richard Pryor might be the funniest guy tonight, but Robert Klein could be the funniest guy tomorrow night. It just depends on how hot they are on any given night and what the audience is in the mood for on any given night."

Margie wasn't impressed with the list at all.

“There are exactly four female comedians in the Top 50 and only one in the Top Ten. Are you frigging kidding me?” she said. “You know this list was put together by a bunch of men.”

“There are just so many good comics who aren’t on the list,” Daisy added. “And I don’t know how in the hell you are supposed to rank them. It’s totally subjective.”

The wine was flowing, and everybody was getting into the debate.

Before long, we would be telling our favorite jokes and talking about the best shows we had ever seen. It’s always a good time when a bunch of hams get together and talk shop. If there is one thing that comics love to do, it is to get all serious when it comes to talking about the least serious things on the planet, humor and levity.

"None of these guys was normal," Sly pointed out. "They were all crazy or misfits in some way or another."

Sly had always held that comics were essentially nuts and, as our group went through the list, it was hard to argue with him. Just looking at the Top Ten, one got a very scary picture of the mental health and stability of the world's top comics.

Pryor set himself on fire smoking crack. Carlin struggled with drugs, too. Bruce was arrested and convicted of violating obscenity laws. Allen fell in love with and married his adopted daughter. Rock was a high school dropout. Steve Martin couldn't stay in a marriage. Rodney Dangerfield was a pot head. Bill Cosby cheated on his wife. Roseanne Barr had an overeating problem. And Eddie Murphy got picked up trying to solicit a transvestite.

"Not exactly the Morality All-Star Hall of Fame," I noted.

But sweet Daisy was her usual forgiving self.

"They are no better or worse than the rest of humanity," she said. "We all have our faults. We all have our sins."

Looking around the table at Sly, Daisy and Margie, I could see where each of us was drawing our stage personas from, where we were getting our eccentric looks from, where each of us was trying to make our connection with the comic universe, consciously or not.

Sly had the Richard Pryor, Chris Rock, skinny black guy thing going down really well. Daisy was a Goldie Hawn knock-off. I was the straightest of the lot, very much in the Johnny Carson, Bob Newhart, Bob Hope vein of comedy. And of course, Margie was a man in a dress. Milton Berle started that, but a bunch of other guys have tried it since.

The more things change, the more they stay the same. Comics

are just cheap imitations of those comics who have gone before them. No surprise there. It is that way in most lines of work.

The robberies started again. And this time, the cops were not stopping until they caught their man. I thought this was probably because whoever was doing the robberies decided to get a little rough the last time out, smacking a kid behind the counter at the drug store with something heavy. They thought it might have been a flashlight. So all of us had to go through another round of questioning on our whereabouts. They even called in Roscoe. The only one who got off with no questioning this time was Dylan.

The police were even going back through some of Slosser's videotapes to make sure that we were where we said we were on the nights in question. But I'm not even sure they knew what else to look for.

The latest round of grilling by the cops didn't produce any new leads, as far as we could tell, but I finally found out why they were so fixated on us as a group.

One of the store owners who had been hit told me that a cop had told him that the suspect, although impossible to identify with a ski cap on, had been caught on a security cam in the alleyway behind the building that houses the comedy club.

I never saw this one coming. Donnelly quit at *Trader Joe's* and entered the police academy. Out of nowhere he had decided to become a member of New York's Finest.

I was sure he would do a great job. Donnelly was a hard worker and a natural born authority figure. It's just that I didn't tend to think of Donnelly as policeman material. He struck me as too much of a prankster, too much of a "give a shit," to wear the blue uniform.

But hey, you know what they say? Certain guys are born to be either criminals or law enforcement officers. Donnelly must have fallen into the latter category. The good news was that with that red hair of his, he was going to make a nice looking Irish cop. The chicks would be all over him.

I have to say I was a little disappointed when I first heard the news. No more Donnelly at *Trader Joe's*. I didn't know how that was going to work. He was a such institution there.

It's always rough when you're the friend who has to stay behind. It's always tough when you know that you'll be the one packing up the tomatoes and spraying down the lettuce, while your pal is out spreading his wings in a new direction.

"You'll still come to see my shows, every once in a while, right?"

I asked. He hadn't been to see one in months.

Donnelly nodded and gave me one of those awkward guy hugs, where the bellies sort of bump up against each other, and the arms don't fully encircle their intended targets.

"Good luck to you man," Donnelly said. "See you round."

He turned to walk away, but swung back a second later with his patented, cool guy smile. "Stay in touch, sport," he said, pausing for a moment. "And make 'em laugh."

Then he was gone.

You could have knocked me and the gang over with a feather.

Mona was getting married to some guy who came into the club

all the time.

Nobody even knew they were dating. And with the man-hating routine that was the hallmark of Mona's on-stage performance, we didn't think she was capable of having a meaningful relationship with anyone of the opposite sex.

Everybody wished her well. She seemed really happy and he seemed like a really good guy who would treat her decently. It was also clear that she had become really eager to get out of the comedy business and start being a housewife. As frequently happens with comics, she had had enough.

It looked like she was going to be set up pretty well. The beau in question was a hunk, made a great living on Wall Street and bought her a diamond ring the size of Roscoe's head. Daisy and Margie couldn't stop ogling the damn thing all day.

“Do you think the cops are going to find anything by looking at Slosser’s videotapes, Dylan?”

I was making small talk before dinner.

“I don’t think so, Dad,” Dylan said. “The tapes aren’t very good.”

“They aren’t very good? Why not?”

“They don’t tell the truth,” Dylan said matter-of-factly.

“Why don’t they tell the truth, son?”

“Because they don’t show what really happened.”

“How can that be?” I asked, puzzled. “Slosser just shoots what’s on stage. How can that not be the truth?”

"Because I saw your routine last night and I saw your mistake," Dylan said.

"What do you mean my mistake?"

"You flubbed your *'the Hudson tastes like chicken'* line on stage," he said.

"Okay," I said, "So what? Comics make mistakes just like everyone else."

"I know, but that's the strange part. That's the part that doesn't make sense to me," Dylan continued.

"Why, Dylan?"

"Your mistake didn't show up on Slosser's tape, the one he showed the police officers later on," he said.

"What?"

"It wasn't on the tape that Slosser showed...."

"No, I heard that," I stopped him. "I just can't believe Slosser showed the police a tape that was wrong."

I looked carefully at Dylan, closely.

"Are you sure the tape didn't have me making a mistake, flubbing my line?"

Dylan looked at me like I had two heads.

"Of course, Dad. I know what I saw," and then he added. "I think we need to tell the police."

Chapter Thirty-One

When the police reviewed the tape, they found out something very interesting. They found out Dylan was right.

There was something amiss with Slosser's tape. He had doctored it. Because he wasn't there to shoot me, he had edited in one of my other performances from another night to cover up for the fact that he had left the video room when I was on stage, left the video room while Dylan was helping Mona out up front.

I guess the cops had been kind of closing in on Slosser anyway, since he was the only one who worked in a room with its own exit to the street. The video room actually had a tiny door that led to the alleyway.

But it was Dylan's detective work that really cracked open the case. Only his remarkable memory of his dad's nightly performances, plus those of the other comics, would have picked up on the video switch.

The police were totally impressed by Dylan's secret talent, his ability to pick up on a clue that they had missed entirely, his ability to see what was really going on, like seeing a woman in a gorilla suit during a basketball game.

They were so impressed that they asked me if they could have Dylan take a look at some other cases that they were having problems cracking. Dylan, of course, was over the moon, couldn't wait to go down to the police station and help out.

Slosser obviously had to go down to the police station too. It made me profoundly sad. I had always thought that Slosser was a good guy, a bit of a loner, but a good guy. Slosser had always been helpful to me, and especially to Dylan. I always considered him a friend. It never occurred to me he could do something outside the law, like commit a robbery.

As it turned out, Slosser had a bit of a gambling problem, and that was probably part of what led to the robberies, that and the sorry state of the comedy business, at least our part of the comedy business. We knew we were the guys on the lower rung of the comedy ladder, guys who weren't ever likely to climb any higher.

We also knew it was getting harder and harder to make ends meet ,for all of us. It was getting harder and harder for us to just laugh off the state of our finances, the state of our lives.

Because it was his first offense and because he didn't have a firearm under his jacket, just his finger, Slosser ended up getting only three years in jail. We heard through the grapevine later on that he got out of prison for good behavior after only one year.

No one from the club ever saw him again.

"Will you take over my nights?" Mona asked. "The Friday and Saturday night rooms?"

I should have seen it coming, but I didn't. Mona was getting hitched to a guy of means. She would be living a different kind of life now. No more struggling to make ends meet for her.

"Let me think about it," I said, mostly because I was in shock and didn't know what else to say.

"What's there to think about?" Mona asked, in her usual sarcastic way. "You'll have to work harder, but you'll be making three times the money you are now."

She had a point. She was not asking me to buy her out. She just wanted somebody to look after what she had built up over the years and to take care of our little comedic family. I was the most logical candidate.

“Yes,” I said, with an enormous grin. “Of course I will.” And then added, “Thanks, Mona. Thanks a lot. It means the world.” She shrugged, but I knew inside she was delighted.

The next day, I quit my job at *Trader Joe’s* and started my life as a full-fledged entertainment executive. Free at last, free at last.

Chapter Thirty-Two

It was quite a field trip, all the way down to Cape May to see Dylan and Suzanne in their play.

It was held in The Village Down Company Theater, as cute a playhouse as a neo-Victorian town can produce on a late summer's eve. The play was called "The Autism Monologues" and it was written, directed and performed by a company of autistic adults, some very high-functioning, others much less so.

Most of the actors, including Dylan and Suzanne, were brutally honest. Some were, quite frankly, angry.

Dylan gave a goose pimple-inducing performance about what it was like to go from being a cute, admittedly different, little kid, a tow-headed, blue-eyed Abercrombie & Fitch ad, to becoming a big hairy ape of a man, with a deep voice, taller than his father, dying to do all the things all young men want to do, drive a car, hold down a job, find a woman who will love them, but not having a clue as to how to do any of these things.

I was spellbound by Dylan's performance. I couldn't have been more surprised, or more proud.

But each of the thespians had their own version of the same story, heart-rending tales of what it was like to try to fit into a world they didn't understand, a world that was not even pretending to try to understand them.

At the end of the play, Dylan, who was now closing in on 16 years of age, read a poem that had been written by a severely autistic boy. The boy had spent his entire life trying to communicate through strange, guttural, jungle sounds. As a result, society had basically dismissed him as little more than an animal. That is until two years ago when the boy typed out a message to his mother using an alphabet board.

"I love you, Mommy," the message said. Then everyone suddenly realized that there was a real, live, intelligent being inside that animal, a real, live, intelligent being trying to get out. Now, at age 10, that same boy was writing breath-taking, awe-inspiring, jaw-dropping poetry, poetry so good it would make William Blake gasp.

"I was reading your mind right now," Dylan's voice rang out in the tiny concert hall, as he quoted the words of the speechless poet. "And the world is as it should be. My world is a soul ride to the life inside my mind."

And when the whole performance was over, the little poet's father, in something of a surprise, took the stage and told the audience that his son had tapped out a message on the alphabet board that he wanted all of them to hear.

"Daddy... Tell the people that no one is normal," the young boy said through his father.

"Daddy... Tell the people that normal is just the average of all of us."

I couldn't believe it. The police department hired Dylan part-time to work for them. They were actually bending the rules somehow and finding a way for him to work for them on weekends even though he was barely old enough to have a driver's license.

The captain down at the station told me that Dylan wouldn't actually get paid until he turned 17. But the head cop said that he thought my son might actually be high-functioning enough to get a full-time job on the police force when he was a little older.

All the guys down at the station house were tutoring Dylan so that he'd be able to pass the test required to be a cop in due course. They figured if they just kept going over stuff with him, his photographic memory would kick in and he would be able to pass the exam with flying colors.

And they weren't just doing it as some kind of charity deal. They were all really impressed when Dylan cracked the Slosser case, and they thought he would be a great asset to their unit.

Donnelly was a full-fledged New York cop by now and coaching Dylan, along with everyone else on the force. Donnelly and Dylan had always gotten along and I thought it was good to have Donnelly more actively involved in my life again too, even if it was primarily through my kid.

I felt so much peace, seeing the possibility that Dylan might actually be able to look after himself at some point in his life. It meant the world to me.

My son, the cop. Who would have thought?

Once again, life truly is stranger than fiction. Guess who is having a baby?

Sly and Daisy.

They are both so excited they can barely contain themselves. They think it is a boy, but they are refusing to let the doctor tell them what flavor it is. They want to wait and see.

What's more, Sly popped the question to Daisy at a party at my apartment a while back. Of course, she said yes without hesitation.

Sly has gone to work for Honda as a salesman and is doing extremely well and Daisy got promoted at TGIF to night manager or something like that, and is really looking forward to doing the whole motherhood thing.

Both of them have packed in stand-up comedy. They say it is just too much for them right now, that they don't have the time to devote to it. But they insist they may come back to it sometime. But I know once a comedian leaves the circuit, he is not coming back. Just doesn't happen.

Funnily enough, Margie dropped out of the comedy circus too. She decided to focus full-time on her telemarketing gig, that and hanging out with Dylan whenever he's around, which isn't all that much.

With all his acting, his homework, his weekend police activity and, most of all, his girlfriend, Dylan has pretty much stopped coming by the club at nights. I miss the hell out of him at work. But at least I get to see him at home sometimes.

It is basically just Roscoe and me left now from the old crowd. I don't think Roscoe will ever quit. He just loves the comedy scene too much, and he has enough money from his lucrative day job that he doesn't need to live off his comedy.

You'll never believe it. You know what Roscoe did for me?

He arranged for me to get a small business loan from his bank, which, in turn, allowed me to do something I never thought I would be able to do. I bought the Big Apple Comedy Club.

What do you know? Clown Boy makes good.

It is a lot of work, and a royal pain in the ass sometimes. But it is a living, and I'm working in the industry I love. How many people can say that?

I know I will never get rich, but I make a lot more than I did when I was just running rooms and moving produce. And I don't mind the hard work. In fact, I kind of like it.

This is not how I saw my life going when I first met Lettie in the spinach section at *Trader Joe's* and fell in love with her. It certainly was not my plan to put myself through the pain of losing her. And I never would have guessed that I would raise my autistic son with the help of a transgender woman whom I've grown to love and respect as much as anyone I've ever known.

No, these are not the kind of things that one dreams about when one is starting up the ladder of life. But sometimes life actually turns out better than one might have expected, turns out better than one might have dreamed.

But enough with the philosophizing.

Tonight, Dylan, Margie and I will stretch out on our oversized couch, under our furry wool blanket, and settle in for a night of watching an old favorite.

After all, who doesn't like *Snow White and The Seven Dwarfs?*

Made in the USA
Middletown, DE
25 June 2019